A PRISONER WITHIN

A PRISONER WITHIN

J.M. Northup

Published 2014 by Creativia
Paperback design by Creativia (www.creativia.org)
Cover art by http://www.thecovercollection.com/
ISBN: 978-1500232023

For Katerina & Desirae
See, I can write dark stories too and this story depicts
the scariest kind of monsters I know.
Sorry, no zombies though

ACKNOWLEDGMENTS

I would like to thank "the other J. Northup" for her generosity of time and talent!

My sister-in-law has provided me with constant support and encouragement. Despite her busy schedule, she edited this novel so I could provide the best product possible to my readers.

CONTENTS

PROLOGUE

"Forgive, but do not forget, or you will be hurt again. Forgiving changed the perspectives. Forgetting loses the lesson."

- Author unknown

CHAPTER ONE

I stood there, battling with myself. The various pieces of silverware seemed weighty as I held them in my hand. My grip was so tight, as my eyes constantly darted to the sharp knives which lay inches from me in the drawer. It was a minuscule space that I could cross in a fraction of a second.

She was so small compared to me. I was young and strong. I couldn't understand why she'd be so cruel or so hateful, especially when I could so easily overcome her. I couldn't fathom what any child could do to make their mother despise them the way she despised me. The venom in her eyes was like a physical blow and her words stung like acid.

I had only wanted to please her; to be close to her. I worked to do things that would make her smile or laugh. All that seemed for naught. Nothing was ever good enough; I was eternally flawed. I wondered why she had kept me if I was the life-ending leech she said I was.

As her screaming droned on, all I wanted was to end her reign of tyranny. In that moment, it wouldn't matter if that meant I had to kill her. It'd be so easy to just grab a knife, turn, and cut her from my life. I envisioned my lethal strike, as I stood shaking, trying to maintain control.

I felt a thrill at the idea of slicing into her body. I didn't care if I did it with a knife or not. Hell, I would've settled for any of the utensils in my hands, even the spoons. They'd all manage my desired goal and bring the anticipated damage I so wanted to reap. It might take a little more force, exerting a bit more effort, but every piece of silverware would inflict harm.

As I stood battling the desire to attack, she continued her ranting; yelling insults at me as she threatened me. She didn't seem to care what she said or did, as long as it hurt me. Her aim was to wear me down. Whether she was truly oblivious to my desires or just that confident that I wouldn't move into action against her, I wasn't sure. All I knew was that she wanted control and submission. Her goal was to break me into giving her just that.

I don't abide by the idea of ruling by fear. I don't agree that "it is better to be feared than respected." I don't believe you can sustain a civilization built upon the backs of slaves. That creates an undertone of hatred and the hope for rebellion; revenge. Forced servitude isn't the same as offering fealty. Fear births hatred and that yields such dark, seedy things that I couldn't see why anyone wanted to use that as a motivator for anything.

Love is the power that is eternal. Even if your ends are wicked, if your means are filled with kindness and warmth, masses will flock to please you. They will gratefully give you what you ask for and do so with a sense of joy. Hasn't history shown us that time and time again? Of course, I wouldn't intentionally use love for personal gain, but I knew my mother would. If she had the capacity or understanding to do so, she'd wield love as her most prized weapon.

So I realized I was at a crossroads. Did I allow my mom's evil to swallow my love and provoke me into darkness? Did I ignore who I was and allow my actions to be hers; literally becoming a person I knew I wasn't? Talking to her was futile; she never listened. I wasn't sure if that was because she didn't really care or because she was arrogant enough to think she was the only one right in the world. I didn't think the answer really mattered, as nothing was going to change simply because she didn't want anything to change.

You can't change a person unless they allow it. You can only control your own behavior and hope that you can offer a good example to influence others. Just like with therapy – or anything really – if a person isn't willing to put forth an effort to try to modify, better, or adjust their reactions, their situation, or their ideas, then all attempts to force a change is futile. Change is personal and entirely dependent upon one person – yourself.

No, I wouldn't compromise who I was. I placed the silverware into its proper place within the drawer. I shut the drawer, hiding away the knives that called to me with such loud voices. I refused to sacrifice my life for a heat of the moment crime. I wouldn't allow her to win. Giving in would feel great, but then, it would ultimately destroy me; making me everything I hated about her. No, I was strong enough to back away and take her abuse. No matter what she did, I wouldn't reciprocate; not today.

"Treat people the way you want to be treated." I lived by that rule. I'd never be like her, if I could prevent it. I'd never purposely make someone feel the way she made me feel. I wanted to on some primal level. I knew I'd be horrified at how much pleasure I'd have if I could watch her life slip away, knowing she was fully aware that it was me who took it. No matter how badly I wanted to drain the blood from her, I knew I'd never attack. God said to be kind and compassionate. That meant I'd never raise my hand against her; at least not intentionally or with premeditation.

As I tried to avoid eye contact, I continued to put away the clean dishes and began washing the new piles. She watched me with a sour look, wanting me to challenge her authority so she'd have a reason to knock me back down. I acted as docile and obedient as I could manage. I apologized and agreed with everything she expected me to support her on – which was how useless and ungrateful I was.

I knew that if I did anything to provoke her, I'd have more to deal with than her irritation. Her displeasure in my ability to execute my chores in a more expeditious manner was more than enough. If her initial anger wasn't immediately abated or her attention redirected, she'd watch me the whole time I washed the dishes. She'd take note of everything she felt I did wrong and use that as her ammunition against me when she'd inspect the dishes for cleanliness. No matter how clean the dishes were in reality, she'd ensure I washed everything again.

If my re-clean didn't appease her and she continued to be angry, I'd be screamed at while having to wash every dish, cup, pot, pan, and utensil in the kitchen. Sometimes she would burn her energy out when I got that far with things, but other times, she'd just build to a crescendo. That would mean I was required to stand at attention, like a soldier, watching my mother as she washed everything herself; which she would do in full insult mode and at max volume.

What hell that would be; too long a night for me. I prayed that my mom would stop short tonight. I hoped there was something on television she wanted to watch or that someone would call her, distracting her. If I were really lucky, she'd be impressed with the program or call and it would catapult her into a good mood; well as good as could be expected for her. That would mean I could slip into bed, feigning sleep for an escape.

Once I'd finished putting away the clean dishes from the dish rack, I worked diligently to prep the kitchen for dish washing. I disposed of the leftovers from the meal under my mother's strict direction, then began to organize the dishes and pre-clean the sink and surfaces. I did everything thoroughly and deliberately in order to avoid more drama. If I was going to be yelled at, I'd rather it be a result of being slow opposed to doing things poorly.

I scraped and rinsed the dishes, stacking them in an orderly fashion on the counter so my mom would understand that I knew the proper order in which to wash things. It was ingrained in me that you soaked the silverware while you washed the glasses and cups. Next, you washed the bowls, followed by the plates. Once you accomplished that, you washed and rinsed the silverware and cooking utensils. At that point, the water would be too dirty to be of any use, so you had to empty the dish pan and rewash the sink, refilling the dish pan before you began to wash the pots and pans.

I meticulously scrubbed the sink and dish pan while my mother watched attentively. I hoped she'd be comforted by my organization and preparations. I hoped she recognized that I was smart enough to know that you didn't wash dishes in a dirty sink. I hoped she'd leave me to my task.

"Make sure that you clean that sink good. You can't clean dishes if you wash and rinse them in filth." Her voice dripped with disgust. I was doing all she asked, so why was she still so angry at me? What was I doing wrong?

I just wanted her to walk away, to leave the room. I just wanted to be invisible so she'd forget about me. I dropped the silverware into the dish pan as I filled it with hot, soapy water and mentally chanted, "Please leave. Please leave."

"Make sure you use hot water!" my mother screamed. "It needs to be so hot that you can barely stand it or it won't get all the germs and shit off."

"Yes, mom," I acknowledged so she knew I was paying attention.

"Your skin should turn red, it's so hot," mother bellowed. She stomped over to test the water temperature to ensure I followed her instructions.

I looked at the stove in disgust, seeing all the food that had baked onto it. I couldn't understand why my step-dad never wiped up his spills when they happened during cooking. If he did then it wouldn't get baked on. I wouldn't have to work so hard to scrape and clean the stove. I felt certain he did it on purpose; perhaps a gesture of disrespect. I wasn't sure if he really disliked me that much or if he just enjoyed my mother's performance as an overlord.

"This stove better shine when you're finished. I don't want any of your lazy shit!" my mom snapped. "Either do it right, or don't do it at all!"

I'd heard it before. It was pretty much the same scene every night. I didn't think that her tantrums were very good for her digestion, but she never seemed to suffer any ill effects from them. The best that I could wish for was that she'd become tired of the usual rampage and walk away. I continued my silent chant, "Please leave. Please leave."

"You *will* do it right." My mother said this as though I seriously thought I had a choice in the matter.

My mother's threat wasn't hollow. I knew things would be done right or at least right in accordance with her standards. I just wasn't sure how many dishes would have to be washed before that was accomplished. To my surprise, it seemed as though my mother was losing interest in our nightly ritual as she called to my step-dad to see if their movie was ready to start. I felt a sense of excitement, delighted with the prospect of something that would divert her attention away from me.

When my step-dad informed her that the movie was about to begin, she gave me one last look of warning, saying, "Get it done."

I felt a wave of relief wash over me as my mother finally existed the room. I sighed deeply, though quietly, so no one would hear. I now dared to hope that I'd be able to cower in the dark of my room sooner rather than later.

I hated living on egg shells. I hated that I didn't have a voice. I hated being nothing.

***

There was a funny smell. I'd been moved around so much that I felt tired and a little disoriented. I vaguely remembered the blur of lights and sounds as I had traveled. Ultimately, I ended up here, in this small quiet room; naked.

"Do you know where you are?" the lady asked me calmly.

"What?" I could hear her voice, but the information wasn't being processed. I was distracted by her lovely red hair; it was so thick and curly. It wasn't that clown color red either. It was that lovely deep auburn with the golden halo that brought the red more to the forefront. I had always loved red hair and dreamt of having a beautiful daughter with lovely red locks and intense green eyes. I wondered what color the talking woman's eyes were.

"Tiffany? Do you know where you are?" the lady asked again with more conviction. I looked directly at her. Of course, I had to; how else would I see the color of her eyes?

"I'm a little cold," I complained mildly. I still couldn't figure out why I was naked. Of course, I wasn't overly concerned about it either; I was trying to see the lady's eye color. I bobbed and weaved to try to follow the lady and I grew agitated that she wouldn't stay still or look directly at me. Why wasn't she being cooperative?

Brown; her eyes were brown. I loved brown eyes best, but I always thought that was too ordinary for my imagined daughter. I wanted her to have striking, vivid eyes of green; a green so intense it made people think she was wearing contacts. My precious child would have such unique eyes that people would think they were inhuman. They would radiate; she'd radiate in gold, amber, and jade. She'd be my jewels; my treasure.

Another woman grasped my arm just above the wrist and asked in a very direct, authoritative voice, "Tiffany. Tiffany, do you know where you are?"

I slowly turned toward this new voice. I wasn't sure whether she sounded angry or just determined. I wanted to look at her face so I could decide; I needed context from her body language. I didn't know what she had to be upset about; I was the one with no clothes to speak of. Upon inspection, I was content to see that the woman didn't appear mad, rather just extremely focused.

This new woman was a bit huskier and a little older than the other lady. She had her hair cut short and I admired the feathering displayed in her golden locks. She wasn't beautiful, but she wasn't ugly either. I did note that she was very strong; her grip was tight and firm. Her voice was deeper than the petite redhead and it caught my attention sufficiently that I began to concentrate better on the conversation.

"What?" I asked her. "What did you say?"

The woman smiled kindly at me and I instantly felt better. I was relieved that she wasn't angry and I was encouraged by her outward display of friendliness. Her smile was warm and it made her ordinary face look extraordinarily pretty. I smiled back at her, hoping my smile was just as lovely. I was certain it wasn't, but I smiled anyway.

"Tiffany, do you know where you are, dear?" the woman asked me quite deliberately this time.

"Yes," I responded to the older woman. "I'm in a hospital."

I looked around me to make sure I'd given the correct answer. The dingy, white room with soft blue and green accents – soothing colors, I acknowledged; to calm a patient – was affirmation enough for me. It also made me understand why I was so drawn to the splash of color the pretty redhead provided in the sea of mundane décor. I immediately returned my attention from the blasé room to the beautiful color.

"Correct," the older woman replied with a hint of relief in her voice.

The two women were turning me about so they could look at my body from every angle. When they looked at my thighs for a long moment, I looked too. I wasn't sure what they were trying to find, but I didn't see anything. The only thing I did see was the bright blood that was smeared across my left forearm. It was quite noticeable in the boringly sterile room. Still, it didn't have the appeal of the lovely hair that tickled when it accidently draped across my skin.

"I don't see any other cuts or abrasions, do you?" The voice was so sweet and the pitch reminded me of something. I just couldn't put my finger on exactly what that something was.

"Me either," I heard the attractively deep voice say.

"Me either," I echoed and then smiled, hoping the ordinary lady would flash her extraordinary smile back at me in return.

"Tiffany, do you have any cuts or wounds other than the one on your arm?" the deep voice demanded kindly.

As I answered, I realized they must be checking me for additional damage. "No. No, I don't think so. Why, did you find something else?"

I began to reassess myself. I still didn't see anything so I wasn't certain what the women were worried about. I was sure that the ER staff had already handled this very thing. After all, hadn't they cleaned, stitched, and bandaged my arm? Looking at my arm, I saw the hint of blood staining the bandages. The blood was a little concerning, I suppose, since it was visible through the wrap, but it wasn't so much that it provided any real reason for alarm.

I noticed the two women looking at each other briefly. I didn't think I would've noticed or cared except that the motion of moving her head made the lady's soft red curls bounce and sway. I liked how even the horrible florescent lights made her hair shimmer with copper. I just knew that it'd be breathtaking to see in the natural light of the sun. I was about to ask her if we could go outside when I detected another question directed my way.

"Honey, do you know why you're here?" Oh, the cute redhead was talking again. A hummingbird, that was it; her voice was like a hummingbird. It was sort of high pitched and small, especially compared to the other woman. I realized I preferred the deeper voice.

"Yes, someone tried to kill me," I answered very matter-of-factly.

CHAPTER TWO

I will never forget that I was born to serve my mother. I'll never forget because she won't let me forget; ever. She reminds me every day that she gave me life, so my life is hers. She owns me; therefore, everything I own is hers by default. I am to do what she wants, when she wants, and how she wants for the duration of her life. That is her due for birthing me.

Sometimes, I think how lovely it would've been to just not exist. I reckon if I were to just disappear now, it wouldn't be me that she'd actually miss, but the servant she sees me to be. I am a jewel to her, not because I am her precious daughter, but because I am a tool to use. Is this really all I am? Is this really my only worth and purpose?

My mother acts very wise about matters of faith, though we do not attend church. I can't recall ever seeing her reading a Bible either, despite having several copies of it around the house. At any rate, she tells me that God commands me to "honor my father and mother". Of course, in her mind, God really means "honor my mother" and condemn my father to hell.

My father was never in the picture; just my step-dad, who married my mom when I was seven years old. I didn't know very much about my biological dad, except that he was the spawn of Satan. My mom didn't really talk about my father much and when she did, she never had anything positive or

reassuring to say. Apparently, I was a chip off his block because I was a devil spawn too.

Even if my father had been around, it probably wouldn't
have helped matters at all. His presence would just have com-
plicated things and given my mom another rival in life. He
would have been another thorn in her side that offered her
another thing to be pissed at me for. If he was really as bad
as she said, perhaps life would have been worse and perhaps
they both would have enjoyed using me as a punching bag.

Then again, my mother tends to be over-dramatic and a
bit pretentious. I mean, she does tell me how blessed I am to
have her, to protect and love me though I know that is a falsehood. With her kind of love and protection, I think I'd be able
to handle whatever evil my father represented. Compared to
her, how much worse could he be?

Before my grandma died, I had asked her about my biological father. Grandma had told me she didn't know who he
was. She said my mother had been very promiscuous and
she doubted my mother really knew who he was either. There
were a few contenders, but paternity had never been verified.
I honestly think my mother preferred it that way though, as
that allowed her to be in total control.

Grandma had told me that my mom always insisted it was
the guy she'd been dating, but he denied it. His said he'd
caught my mom with another man and that he refused to
raise me or be involved with me since he'd never be sure I
was his. He refused to take a paternity test, saying that was
insulting and degrading. Had my mother received help from
the state then the courts could have ordered paternity tests,
forcing the prospects to submit results. I figured my mother's
need to have complete authority was why she never forced
the issue.

My grandma had been a proud woman and she refused to
allow my mother to partake in any welfare programs. I was

sure that was where my mother's determination and stubbornness had come from. Of course, in the end, it was best that it had played out like it did. Not having to worry about my biological father allowed my step-dad to easily adopt me. Still, the adoption didn't make him a real parent or a real father. Adoption didn't negate my mother's dominance and the honor she expected for being a mother.

You know, honor is like respect. I'd have no problem honoring either my mother or my step-dad - respecting them even - if only they'd honor and respect me in the same way. Doesn't it all go back to treating people the way you want to be treated? I mean, if you want me to be nice to you, shouldn't you be nice to me? Why do some people receive exemption from this; and who gave them the authority to decide their exemption?

I wished my mother would treat me the way she treated our dog. I knew she loved that fucking dog more than anyone or anything else in the world. Sometimes I even wondered if the dog was the one thing she actually did loved besides her own self. How could I make her love me like that? Of course, I would settle for her just leaving me alone, especially right now. Please leave me alone.

"What the hell is wrong with you?" she was asking in an ugly tone. "Why can't you do anything right? You're fucking useless!"

It really didn't matter what my mom had tasked me with; regardless of the chore, I'd always be incompetent for the job. When I was a little girl, I had just wanted to please my mom. I just wanted her approval. Now, I understood that I could never please her and her approval was unattainable. In some ways, knowing this made her words less hurtful, but the sting was undeniable and her words still hurt.

I was beating the section of carpet that was left on the porch for our dog to lie on. Since most of the yard was exposed earth, void of grass due to our large ass dog tearing it up repeatedly, the carpet was caked in dried mud. My mother had decided today was a good day for me to clean the porch which was actually the dog's house.

My mother had rescued our dog from a neighbor who ignored the leash law and let the dog run loose through the neighborhood. My mother tired of seeing the neglected dog roaming around, hungry and dirty, so she brought him home. My mother had words with the neighbor and eventually, the neighbor tired of my mother's commentaries and opted to move away, leaving the dog behind.

With my mother's obsessive-compulsive tendencies, she was not able to have the dog live inside the house with us. Being an animal lover, she couldn't bear the idea of making the poor creature live outside in the southeastern Texas weather either. Her solution was to convert half of our large, covered back patio into an oversized dog house. It was really nice for the dog, but it sucked for me.

The back door opened to a decent-sized yard that was surrounded by a black iron-barred fence. This fence marked our yard, separating it from the yards on either side of us and from the walking trails around the pond behind our houses. With people frequently passing by and being able to see into our yard with visibility to the back patio, my mother insisted that it remain immaculately clean. That made this one of her favorite ways of punishing me while giving her an excuse to enjoy the sunshine and time outside with her dog.

The dog was extremely pampered and my mother enjoyed sunbathing with the lazy creature. My mom loved the dog so much that she overlooked the damage it caused to our yard as well as the smell of its excrement as it baked in the sun. My step-dad had enclosed a portion of the patio, not only to form the homemade dog house, but to regulate its temperature as well. My mother insisted that there be a doggy door that would maintain the cold air from the installed air conditioner during the hot Houston summers. In order to make the dog more comfortable against the exposed cement, carpet was laid down. Hence, the reason my chore existed.

I hated that stupid piece of carpeting. I couldn't fathom how a person would think it possible to shake the damn thing. I resented that chore and more so, I resented my mom's affinity for our dog. It was hard to know she loved that critter more than she loved me. Though I loved our dog too, I was angry and extremely bitter. Shouldn't a mother love her child more than her pet?

I knew it was wrong to blame the dog; it was my mom who'd created the situation. Still, I tended to shy away from the dog. It was more than the fact that I was a cat person; it was because I knew the dog came first. I knew that in the ranking of our house, the dog ruled over me. I didn't want to punish the dog with misdirected emotions, so I just stayed away from it altogether.

My mother was beyond irritated. Apparently, I hadn't hung the section of carpet on the clothes line properly. Then I wasn't striking the rug correctly; either I was hitting it from the wrong angle or I wasn't hitting it with enough force. I knew the truth was that she wanted to complain and it didn't matter what I did; nothing would be good enough.

When my mother finally stomped off in a cloud of exasperation, I sighed quietly. I looked at the carpet with annoyance. No matter how hard or how long I struck the piece, I'd never get the dirt and grime out of it and certainly not to my mother's standards. I knew that I was screwed no matter what I did and that I'd have a difficult night ahead of me.

I felt angry and hurt. I felt small and insignificant. In that moment, my mother's words stung with truth in my ears. I was useless. I was powerless to change my life and the circumstances that left me in a state of fear and dread. People say, "Life is what you make it," but I couldn't see that. I certainly didn't choose to make my life the way it was.

Feeling overwhelmed and stuck, I lashed out with great strength. I beat the carpet with all I had, repeatedly. I pounded out my pain and the feel of the mud chunks flying off, striking my body with force, only pushed me to exert more energy. When I was finally spent, I relaxed as I stood back to assess my work. I was breathing hard, but it felt good to have released some of the tension from my body; I felt emotionally lighter, as well.

For that one calming moment, I almost found a sense of peace. That was until my mother's hand struck me on the back of my head. The unexpected blow threw me forward and I barely caught myself before I fell into the dirt.

"You lazy, useless bitch," my mother snapped. "What are you doing just standing there?"

I looked at her with open surprise. I was too shocked to mask my response. I failed to hide my expression or body language. I gaped at her until her look finally penetrated my brain, warning me that I was in danger. As quickly as I could, I regained my composure and apologized for whatever she thought I'd done, or hadn't done.

"Leave it to you to be standing around when there's work to be done," she accused rudely. "I can't even let you alone to get myself a drink." She clicked her tongue in disgust.

I apologized again and looked at the ground with chagrin. This seemed to appease her, so I continued to avoid eye contact. Perhaps she was like a wild animal – making eye contact was a sign of aggression; a sign of challenge. Maybe if I kept my eyes averted, I'd get through this with minimal trouble.

As she sipped on her tea, she pointed to the patio saying, "I want shit done; *now!*"

As I turned my attention back to the porch, I could hear her complaining loudly about the "piss poor" job I'd done. A spark of anger hit me and I wanted to yell at her to do stuff her damn self. Of course, I knew what the consequences would be if I did that, so I kept my temper along with keeping my mouth shut. An overwhelming sadness pervaded me, stalling me in my efforts to sweep. I swallowed hard, fighting my tears and stifling a soft, muffled cry; it almost sounded like a frog croaking.

My mother abruptly looked in my direction. In an effort to misrepresent the sound, I put my hand to my mouth and said, "Excuse me."

It worked; she assumed I'd burped or something equally gross to her. She walked away disgusted with me, settling into her lounge chair to sun-bathe. All the while, bitching aloud about my inept abilities and crude behavior. As she took her seat on the extended cement patio that encircled our small pool, the neighbor's walked up through their yard from the trails. They called greetings to my mother who returned their salutations with an air of pleasantness.

Never missing the opportunity to build her public appearance, my mother got up from her lounge chair and started walking over to the fence that separated our yard from the neighbor's yard. It was a simple iron fence, but greenery and Crepe Myrtles had been planted along its length in an attempt to make the yards a bit more private. Perhaps the vegetation was also an attempt at making the yards look prettier too, but I couldn't see it; this place was nothing but ugly to my eyes.

Our one-story home with its covered, partially enclosed back patio and front veranda was nothing more than a prison to me. The dirty yard and weathered pool were an eye-sore, though my mother was proud of them; mostly because we were one of the few homes in the community to have our own pool. I knew I should be more grateful for the blessings I had, especially when so many others went without. Still, I doubted I'd ever think of this place fondly. At any rate, there existed an open viewing into each other's yards that forced my mother to mind her manners.

My mother didn't mind the exposure; any audience was a delight to her. She wasn't inhibited by the openness of our yards nor the view other's had of my humiliation. My mother actually thrived on the attention and used it to her full advantage, highlighting how difficult it was for her to have me around. She knew how to play on people's emotions and always managed to be rewarded by the ego-stroking she desired.

My mother loved compliments, especially ones about her being courageous enough to raise her daughter with "tough love". My mother basked in the cheers about her not being afraid to discipline me, especially in our society of leniency. My mother always made sure to cast herself as the martyr, while I, of course, was cast as the villain. I was the one who had always done something that forced her hand, provoking whatever punishment I received. People just seemed to eat her bullshit up.

Everyone always supported my mother, though they never heard my side of the story. I forgave them, knowing they were just disillusioned. Most made the mistake of assuming all parents loved their children unconditionally; I reckon they really didn't know any better. Those that did know better either tolerated my mother's behavior to make things easier on me or to avoid confrontation with her. No matter how you looked at it, I couldn't win. People always thought my mom was a terrific mother and I was a juvenile delinquent causing her heartache.

My mother went on a gentle rant about me, keeping it lighthearted so as to not impose too strongly on the neighbor's goodwill as they indulged her mild tirade. According to her speech, I'd been tasked with cleaning the back porch as a way to teach me the value of hard work. This was earned because I apparently didn't appreciate how hard my mother and step-dad worked.

After hearing the short story, the neighbor's excused themselves and started for their house. I could hear the wife say to her husband how sweet my mother was and how badly she felt that my mother had such a troubled child. He agreed with her and added that it was a shame such a good parent had to have such an ungrateful daughter. I wondered how they'd feel if they knew what she was really like.

***

"Do you know who tried to kill you?" It was the lady with the deeper voice; a nurse I now realized.

"Hmmm... what?" I asked, hoping the nurse would talk more. I liked the pitch and cadence of her voice. I wanted to keep looking at the redheaded nurse, but to listen to the huskier, blond one.

"Do you know who tried to kill you, Tiffany?" she asked again.

Just then, someone tapped lightly on the door then popped their head in without waiting for a reply. It was another nurse, I guessed, but her white hair and white scrubs seemed to blend into the room. I lost interest quickly and searched for the pretty red hair again.

"Hey, Rhonda, do you need any help?" the new nurse asked in a dull, uninterested voice. "I'm getting ready to leave and thought I'd ask before I left."

I wanted her to leave. Her voice was just as boring as all her white appearance against the white room. She added nothing of interest, only interruptions. Focusing more intently on the bouncy red hair, I wondered what the texture was like. I wondered if it would be feather light like my own hair or coarse, the way the nurse called Rhonda's hair seemed to be. I instinctively reached up to grasp a curl between my fingers.

Rhonda quickly removed my hand, saying, "No, we're good. You can go; thanks."

"Are you sure?" the white nurse asked, though I could tell she was anxious to get away.

"Ugh," I responded. "Go already."

Again I reached up to grasp the red curls. Again, Rhonda retracted my hand, but this time she caught it before I actually made contact. While the redheaded nurse shushed me softly, Rhonda called back to the white nurse and said, "I'm sure, but can you ask Carol to come in here please? I need to grab a few things and I don't want to leave Charlotte in here alone."

"No problem," the white nurse said and to my relief quickly left, closing the door behind her.

I was so happy she had left; happier still knowing the red-headed nurse's name was Charlotte. That actually made me happy. Charlotte was a name I could see this petite lady with the higher-pitched bird voice having. Charlotte. Yep, I liked it; it suited her. Though I was still uncertain how I felt about Rhonda. I felt she was bettered suited to be called Suzanne.

Thinking about the names of the nurses caused me to start an internal dialogue about names. It brought to mind one of my favorite sitcoms, *The Big Bang Theory,* and the episode where Barry Kripke meets Penny for the first time. In the episode, he tells her that the name Penny isn't a "hot name" so he's going to call her Roxanne instead. This made me chuckle a little. When I thought of the similarities between the two names – Suzanne and Roxanne – I began giggling harder.

I must have startled the nurses with my unexpected laughter. They both jumped a little and Charlotte took a small step backwards. The nurses looked at one another, and Charlotte seemed to be more alarmed when I followed her motion forward and placed my hand on her shoulder. I was using her as a support so I could lean forward as I burst into full on laughter.

It felt so good to laugh. I realized that I didn't laugh enough and I wished that I did. I remember hearing that laughter was supposed to be the best medicine, so why didn't I prescribe that in my life more? Perhaps I would be happier? It was something to ponder for sure.

Realizing the way the uneasy manner of the nurses when subjected to my unexpected laughter, I tried to calm them by explaining the joke. Unfortunately, my laughter made my story unclear and somewhat incoherent. Before I would redeem myself and offer a better explanation, we were interrupted by the nurse called Carol.

Carol knocked gently and came into the room almost simultaneously with the knock. I didn't mind though. She was beautiful! My laughter subsided into intrigue and I was mesmerized by Carol. The caramel color of her skin was radiant and her brown hair was glowing like someone had weaved gold into her hair. Of course, I knew it was the highlights in her hair, but it was a beautiful effect. She reminded me of the performer, Beyoncé Knowles, and that's when I realized Carol was a young black lady. I wished I looked like her; she was a knock out even for a heterosexual female like me.

Carol's voice matched her beauty and I instantly wanted to hear her talk more when she checked in with Rhonda, "Gwen said you needed me?"

"Yes," Rhonda acknowledged. "Can you help Charlotte finish the in-take with this patient so I can ensure her room is available?"

"Sure," Carol readily answered and quickly came forward to relieve Rhonda.

Rhonda smiled kindly at her and said, "Thanks."

"Sure, no problem," Carol returned.

"I'll just be a moment," Rhonda promised.

Much to my relief, Charlotte and Carol began to help me get dressed. I was excited that I was given my own pair of scrubs to wear. I knew they were comfortable and I had always loved scrubs. Plus, I had never been a fan of going commando though, so being without my panties was uncomfortable.

I didn't appreciate having to go without under garments. That just felt odd and frankly, a bit naughty. A gal should have sensible underwear, in my opinion. I mean, I know that it is an old joke for mother's to say "make sure you have clean underwear on in case you're in an accident", but it's not really supposed to be serious, right? I thought about that strange old adage and giggled again. People said the weirdest things.

CHAPTER THREE

"You're a whore," my mother accused cruelly.

I was flabbergasted. How had my mother come to that conclusion? I hadn't even had my first kiss let alone sex before so how could I possibly be a whore? I was barely allowed to leave my house. I was barely allowed to go places in a group with girls, so dating was non-existent.

"Mom, I haven't done anything," I promised. I wanted to placate her, but I wasn't sure if anything I said helped.

"You disgust me," she cried at me like a banshee.

"What did I do wrong? He asked me for my phone number so I gave it to him," I explained.

"That is *my* phone number," my mother screamed. "You have no right to give it out."

I didn't understand. I wasn't following my mother's logic at all. I lived here too and we only had the one house phone. If I needed to call someone or they needed to call me, what other number was I supposed to give? If the phone in my own home wasn't mine to give out then what did that leave me?

I wasn't allowed to have a cell phone. My mother said that I hadn't earned that privilege and she wouldn't waste her money on an ungrateful bitch like me. She told me that she didn't trust me anyway. She knew I'd just stay up all night sexting guys and sending inappropriate pictures or videos, so she wasn't going to enable my sick behavior. No, I didn't deserve such things.

Of course, I'd never engage in such lewd behavior, but it didn't matter. The only thing that mattered was what my mother thought or felt about a situation. Like she said, I didn't get an opinion or say in anything until I was supporting myself and since I wasn't allowed to exist without my mother, I'd never have any contribution worthy of acknowledgement. Besides, it didn't have to be true; it just had to be enough of a reason for my mother to maintain the appearance of being a concerned, responsible parent, especially when she denied me basic things like sleeping in my own bed.

It annoyed me to hear her say things like "sexting" and I wasn't even certain she knew what it really meant. Sexting; she heard the term on some television show and thought it would impress people if she could use it. She thought it made her seem fashionable and hip that she could use current tex-ting vernacular. I just thought it made her seem like an idiot, though I'd never confess that to anyone.

We had a land-line that was intended for the entire family to use. Of course, my mother meant that it was only for me to use for emergencies, business, or as a means for her to track my whereabouts when she wasn't home. She loved to randomly call the house and since we had a caller ID, she'd use different phone so I wouldn't recognize any particular number. The game was to see if I were home, how quickly I answered the phone, and what I sounded like when I did answer. She'd be pissed if she had to wait longer than two rings and she'd be suspicious if I were out of breath.

My mom ensured we didn't have a cordless phone because she didn't want me to have a radius in which to screw around; she wanted to know I was home-bound with certainty. If I had a cordless or cellular phone then I could take it outside or someplace other than my house and she'd never really know. It was easier for her to control me if she could contain me.

My mother also had a knack for calling me while I was in the bathroom. This talent caused me to get yelled at a lot. Of course, mom never believed that I'd been in the latrine and raced to get to the phone in time. My delay and increased breathing was always attributed to some mischievous behavior; usually involving a random boy she'd imagined.

I was baffled by this new turn of events. If I wasn't allowed to give out my mother's number, what did that mean for me? To what extent was the restriction? Did it only apply to personal relationships or did that carry into the professional realm? Should I inform my work that I no longer have a contact number? I was scared to ask for clarification, but I needed to know.

"Does that mean I can't give the number to my work?" I tried to breach the subject to obtain more information, but in a way that would avoid escalating my mother's anger.

Surprisingly, my question seemed to catch my mother off guard. I saw a momentary lapse in her anger and the look of confusion flash across her face. The question had taken her aback sufficiently that she actually looked like she was re-evaluating her stand on the issue and re-processing the conversation at hand. At least, that was what I was hoping her facial expressions were indicating. For all I knew, I could have just tossed more fuel on her fire and revived the craziness.

"Don't be stupid," she finally said.

That really didn't help me with my confusion. I remained quiet, trying to keep a neutral expression on my face, hoping she would elaborate on my stupidity. Thankfully, that was just what she did.

"Of course, you can give the number out to your work," she snapped and I realized a new rage was building in her. "I just don't want you to give it out to *guys.*"

The way she said the word "guys" was chilling. I knew she would have used a more degrading word had she been able to think of one. I couldn't help letting my mind wonder about what other word options she had, but then her tone immediately brought me back to the conversation at hand.

"I don't want a whore for a daughter," my mother said it in a way that expressed great disappointment and disgust; she already thought she had a whore for a daughter.

"I'm sorry," I told her, though I knew I had no reason to apologize. "How does giving my phone number to guys make me a whore?"

I was afraid. I hadn't meant to be so direct with my question. I hadn't really intended to ask her that question at all, actually. The words just slipped out before I could contain them. Now, I waited to see what they would reap.

She looked at me as thought I were stupid and shook her head slightly. She gave a slight *tsk* before saying, "You cheapen yourself by giving your number out to guys. They think you're an easy lay."

I just stared at her. What? In that moment I did feel stupid; I felt an inability to comprehension the logic my mother presented. Surely, I must be missing something because I just couldn't grasp what she meant. Where did she get the idea that giving my phone number to a guy who asked for it meant I was easy? What if we were simply exchanging information in order to work together on a school project? What if I was giving him my phone number because we worked together and we were discussing a schedule change?

"Can I ask them for their number then?" I immediately regretted asking.

My mother looked like she wanted to smack me. I was surprised when she didn't actually do it. I had seen her hand start to move, but she restrained it; making a fist and taking a deep breath. Shit. Now I started to wonder if she was going to punch me instead. Thankfully, she did neither.

"No," she tried to keep calm. She continued to explain things to me as though I was a tiny child and not a young woman of sixteen. "You can't ask for their number because that'd make you loose and forward; they'd think you were chasing them."

Was she serious? Did she really believe this or was this her anger talking? Either way, she sounded crazy to me.

"So, if they ask for my number – *your* number, I mean – then I'm not allowed to give it to them because that'd make me cheap and easy," I asked, trying to word things right and ensure I had complete understanding of the rules. "And I cannot ask for their number because that'd mean I was chasing them?"

"Exactly," she said firmly. She actually looked like she was pleased I was getting it. "And if you're chasing them, well, that's no better than propositioning them. You may as well just lay down with your legs spread open and tell them to fuck you."

I blinked slightly, trying to absorb what she was saying. How did she make the two ideas correlate in her head? Did she really interpret the situation like that? Where did *that* leave me?

I felt confused and frustrated. I never gave my mother any reason to suspect me of any unbecoming behavior. I was a good student and I did everything I was told. I got into enough trouble because of things my mother dreamt up that I didn't actually need to do anything to get punished. Sometimes, she'd punish me for something someone else did, saying that if I knew the punishment then I wouldn't want to do the crime.

I existed in a state of constant fear, guilt, and anxiety. I was always so worried I'd be in trouble that I never attempted to do anything to begin with. I spent all my energy in trying to blend in and disappear. My focus was on avoiding problems instead of creating them. Couldn't she see that? Furthermore, couldn't she see how drastic and ridiculous her summation was?

"I need to go to the bathroom," I said tentatively.

"So go," my mother snapped.

As I made my way into the bathroom, she followed me. I was uncomfortable when my mother was in the latrine with me, but what choice did I have? I certainly didn't want to make a bad situation worse and I really did have to urinate. As I sat down on the toilet, I hoped my mother would simply leave me to my business, though I knew that wasn't going to happen.

My mother was eyeing me in a weird way. She kept moving her head back and forth as she sort of ducked and bobbed. I looked at her inquisitively and with great trepidation. What the hell was she looking at? What was she looking for? Even worse, did she actually see something? I was growing more and more uncomfortable with each passing moment.

"Are you having sex?" she asked me in a hateful voice.

"No," I replied shocked. How had my need to pee turned into sex?

"You know, I can tell if you aren't a virgin," my mother warned. "You may as well tell me because I'll be able to tell if you're fucking around."

My mouth opened in complete disbelief. I realized I had my answer as to what she was looking at – my vagina. Yuck! As to whether she could tell if I'd been sexually active or not didn't worry me; I hadn't been sexually active. I was baffled as to how she thought she could tell though and worried that she'd try to get a closer look.

To my relief she made no attempt to look closer. However, the damage was done; the seed of resentment was sown. I felt violated and dirty. I was deeply offended and thoroughly frustrated that there was nothing I could say or do about it. I hated her in that moment; I hated myself.

I couldn't deny that there was a part of me that felt like saying I was sexually active just to piss her off. Worse, there was that part of me that thought if I was already been accused of it and punished for it, then I should just do it. Of course, I didn't want to be that person. Did I? No, I didn't. I knew who I was and who I wanted to be; neither was the person my mother wanted to portray me as.

Thankfully, my mom got a phone call as I was washing my hands. The caller was someone my mother enjoyed talking to, as she got wrapped up in her conversation. I didn't care who called, but I was grateful they did. They effectively distracted my mother from her tirade and allowed me to escape to the confines of my bedroom. Though my bedroom wouldn't save me from my mother, not seeing or hearing me made her less inclined to interact with me.

***

After I was dressed, Charlotte busied herself with writing on a chart and Carol placed my personal effects into a paper bag. Rhonda and Charlotte had taken detailed accounts of my personal effects and Carol was no less thorough. She annotated my information on the bag. As they finished, Rhonda returned to say my room was ready. I felt excited about that because it meant I could leave this dull little room. I was bored by it so I was happy to have a change of scenery.

As we moved down the hallway, I didn't really pay attention to where we were going. Again, it was just more about flashes of light and color. I was more aware of smells than I was of anything else really. I think we passed by people, but none of them registered in my mind; I'd never recognize them if we were ever to meet again.

I vaguely felt as if I ought to be more alert, but it was a fleeting thought. My mind was both numb and over-active at the same time. Thoughts were jumping around inside my mind just as the light and colors seemed to swirl around me. I wondered if I'd be able to find my way around the hospital. Actually, I started to wonder why I was really in the hospital.

My arm had been attended to by the emergency room attendant. It had been the only notable damage to speak of and though I had bled a lot and was a bit in shock from the wound, it proved to be minor. It had been a clear cut and it had missed anything vital; no tendons, veins, or blood vessels. Though I didn't have a full recollection of how I got to the emergency room or what had transpired while I was there, I knew that much. I also knew that I had stitches and an antibiotic to prevent infection.

With my arm patched up, I was starting to question why I was still at the hospital. I wasn't aware of any additional damage and no one else seemed concerned, so why were they detaining me? Hadn't their examination assured them that I was good to go; perhaps they just didn't want to send me home with my mom?

That must have been it. Surely, I must have told them my account of the incident, though I had no memory of doing so. Thinking harder, I didn't think anyone actually asked me what happened. Well, I must have said something or my control freak mother would have been here the whole time, right? Something seemed off to me.

Just then I was led into a small room. To my surprise, the room was filled with furniture that was made from hard plastic. Everything was made with rounded edges and even the bathroom was designed to prevent injuries. The toilet and sink were made from smooth metal and there were no moveable parts outside of the handles. The shower was open and designed to be a walk-in, so additional fixtures could be avoided; no tub to drown in, I pondered.

Everything was designed for simplicity. The idea seemed to be to remove anything that might promote mischief or inflict harm. There were no cords or strings of any sort and I wasn't allowed to have any of my personal items back if they didn't adhere to the "no strings" policy. I was allowed my sandals back simply because they slipped on. That was nice anyway.

I understood the need to lock-up my personal items so nothing was stolen, but the rest was baffling to me. Did they really think I would strangle myself or someone else if I had shoelaces or hood strings? What kind of person did they think I was?

Crazy; they thought I was crazy. That was when it hit me; I was in the psych ward. I was being detained because they had thought I was a danger of some sort. I tried to consider this new bit of information, but my mind was too scrambled for me to latch onto anything long enough to make much sense of it. I just felt more lost and confused.

There wasn't a phone in the room, but I was told if I wanted to make a call, I could use the phone in the day room. It was shared among all the patients in the ward and was visible from the nurses' station. I assumed that was done on purpose so that calls could be monitored somewhat. I didn't care, as I had no one to call anyway and even if I had, there'd be nothing to say that merited hiding.

All in all, it was a weird set-up. I wasn't sure what to make of it all. Still, it was quiet and I liked the sage color of the walls and the creamy linens. I walked over to the window and looked out blankly. The city lay out in front of me and I could see downtown in full view. I thought about how pretty it'd be at night; lit up like a Christmas tree. That was something to look forward to, especially since it seemed so unattractive to me just then.

I was the room's sole occupant which was probably why it was so angular and small. As a female in a co-ed unit, I wasn't allowed to be partnered with another patient unless there was absolutely no space left. I wondered why that was and then realized I didn't care. It was a benefit to being female that I'd proudly accept; I liked solitude. Besides, I really had no interest in socializing; particularly not that fake niceness and small talk crap required of you in a situation like this.

After the nurses ensured I was comfortable and acclimated to my room, they retreated, leaving me alone. I sighed, allowing a calming breath of relief to wash over me and then I sat down on the low plastic bed. It was odd to be in a hospital without the traditional bed or room apparatus. There wasn't even a television because, as the nurse pointed when she saw my interest in the room, they wanted to encourage us to go to the day room. They wanted to reward socializing because apparently that was good behavior and meant good mental health.

I felt incredibly weary all of a sudden. The bed looked so inviting and it made me realize just how exhausted I was. I couldn't really remember most of what had transpired that day, but it didn't matter. All that mattered was that I could finally lie down and give in to my weariness. As I cuddled into the sheet and blanket, I rested my head on the flat pillow. It was heavenly, as was my imminent escape into slumber.

CHAPTER FOUR

"If you ever try to run from me, I *will* find you and I *will* kill you."

I had no doubt in my mind that my mother meant exactly what she said. It made me feel hopeless and afraid. I didn't feel like I was on stable ground and my faith was shaken to its core. I felt like I had no future; or at least, no control over what my future would be.

I felt stuck and in that moment, I had a profound realization; this battle would never end. It was a fight in which I had never actively participated yet it had raged on for my entire life. It was a battle my mother was engaging in fiercely and one that defined our relationship. The battle was over my life and in the end, there could only be one winner.

I saw it clearly and it filled me with deep sorrow. It would come down to "kill or be killed". My mother would never be satisfied with anything less than total domination; one of us wasn't going to make it out this alive. I briefly wondered who it would be.

I really wasn't a violent person, but I was still my mother's daughter. There was no way in hell I'd go down without a fight; at least that's what I told myself. I hadn't yet tested the truth of that sentiment, but I knew one day I would. When that moment came, I wasn't really convinced that I would fight. I had to admit there were times when I felt tired and the idea of not having to expel so much energy was inviting. I hated having to fight for the right to exist.

Death seemed comforting when I thought of it in terms of escape. The peace that flowed through me almost made me wish for it; it'd be so easy and I was sure my mom would oblige me in any way possible. The idea of peace was enticing enough to at least consider death as an option. Sometimes I thought I'd do my mother the favor and end it all myself. Still, I struggled with the ramifications of suicide; would I really go to hell for it?

I contemplated the concept of hell. What did it mean to me? After living with my mother, would burning for eternity be much worse? I wondered about heaven. Yeah, I didn't like the idea of potentially missing out on heaven for a possible eternity of a similar or worse existence than the one I already knew. No, I wouldn't be seduced by death today.

"Still," I thought to myself with a dark chuckle, "it *would* be better. I mean, at least I'd know what to expect and not live on egg shells anymore."

My mother slapped me hard across the face. I staggered a few steps before I regained my balance. I hadn't expected to be struck at all, let alone across the face. Immediately, I was aware of my error; I had stopped paying attention to my mother's ranting. Damn. I bet she had asked me a direct question and when I didn't respond promptly, she decided to demand my attention in a way that satisfied her; and consequently hurt me. Shit; what did I miss?

My mother believed in turning her rings so the stones would be on the inside of her hand. That way when she struck you, you'd develop a welt on your face; maybe even have a wound from the gem splitting the tender skin. I knew that the satisfaction of hitting me was pleasing enough to my mother, but to leave a noticeable mark was sheer delight. After all, she had trained me well enough to be confident that I'd lie in response to any questions about it.

Mother knew no one would suspect her cruelty. Appearances were everything to her and like the old gangster movies portrayed, we did *not* speak against the family. Our business was our business and anyone nosing around could go fuck themselves. This had been ingrained in me since birth and it was instinct to comply. I was accident-prone by nature, so that helped.

I turned my attention back to my mother, my eyes wide with shock. My hand instinctively went to cover my cheek. It felt hot and it stung. I wondered if I would have a visible mark; I'd be surprised if I didn't. Damn. There'd be a lot of questions at school the next morning. Thankfully, I was a klutz who constantly entertained the masses with my unintentional antics. I bruised easily and everybody knew it. I had a documented propensity to fall down and run into things so it was easy to cover the notable damage with feasible lies.

The irony of the situation didn't escape my attention. I had made enough trips to the ER due to my own awkwardness that no one thought much of it when I was there due to my mother. Since I never spoke against her and generally added to the lies she told, I was an accomplice. I enabled my mother and assured her safe passage as we navigated authority figures and curious on-lookers. Wow; that sucked.

"You'll listen to me when I'm speaking to you," she roared at me. She had a slight smile on her face and in her rage it just made her look more sinister.

"I'm sorry," I said gingerly.

"Oh, you'll be sorry all right," my mother replied.

I felt fear deep in the pit of my stomach. I wasn't sure what was coming and, honestly, that was the worst part. It left me unable to think of ways to try to diffuse the situation or to protect myself. I didn't know what to do to minimize the expected damage to my person. I felt nauseous.

My mother's eyes sparkled. This was pure entertainment to her. She loved having the authority to force me to do her will. She reveled in the power she had over me. She felt absolutely certain that I'd do nothing except show blind obedience, taking whatever she threw at me with grace and as much dignity as the circumstances allowed. After all, that was how she raised me.

I was submissive by habit, and passive by nature. To make things worse, I craved my mother's love and approval so much, that I would probably endure anything to see her happy with me. It was a sick behavior and an unhealthy relationship all around. I felt pathetic and stupid, but that didn't change my reaction to anything.

My mother knew my first instincts were to cower. I'd never run for fear of the repercussions once she caught me, as she had drilled it into my head enough times that she'd "find and kill me". She knew I'd never attack her, as that was foreign to my personality; out of my character. The commandment to "honor thy mother and thy father" was ingrained into my psyche. I'd submit to her will and she'd bask in the joy of it all.

My step-dad was in his usual place at the kitchen table, reading a newspaper as he sipped coffee. He simply ignored our interaction; something I never really understood. I wasn't sure whether his lack of response was out of habit or because he didn't want my mother's wrath directed towards him? Perhaps it was because he really didn't give a damn about me since I wasn't his biological child.

At any rate, his presence did nothing for me. However, it strengthened my mother and reassured her of her power over me despite her small stature. If I ever were to fight back, my mother knew my step-dad would intervene. He was her heavy hand and his promise of force kept me in my place even when the instinct to run was overwhelming.

My step-dad submitted to my mom even more than I did. He obeyed her every wish and it made me sick to my stomach. How could someone sit back and allow a child to be abused? How could he kowtow to a woman like my mother; allowing her to hurt someone he knew to be innocent? If I had been in his position, there was no way I could stand idly by, watching an injustice repeat day after day.

My step-dad was just as bad as my mother; perhaps worse, in my opinion. My mother might have been cruel, but I felt like she truly believed she was trying to make me a better person. I didn't appreciate how she chose to teach me things, but I knew the lessons were priceless. I knew if I made it out of this alive, I would be able to face anything the world threw at me. I couldn't say the same about him.

I was sure people thought of my step-dad as a manly man. After all, he was a strong, robust construction worker. From the outsider's point of view, my step-dad's behavior was attributed to his sense of chivalry. They considered him a gentleman and they interpreted his attentiveness to mom as endearing and loving. They didn't realize the truth.

My step-dad was my mother's servant as much as I was. The difference between us was that he enjoyed serving her. Though we both wanted my mother's approval, he definitely wanted it more than I did; his was a pathological need. He was no man at all by my estimation and the inability for other's to see him as he truly was only made me think of them as ignorant and naïve.

My mother took a step towards me, her hand raised in the air above me, ready to strike. I cowered slightly and tears flowed from my eyes. When my mother registered my reaction to her intentions, she smiled wickedly. Her hand twitched and she looked pensive. I knew she was trying to decide what her next course of action would be. Mercifully, she lowered her arm and started to bark orders at me.

I was thankful that she had decided not to dispense a physical punishment. Instead, she made me scour the house, performing a barrage of chores while she watched me accomplish them to her standards. I knew that my response to her silent physical threat had pleased her, hence the easier, more forgiving punishment. It was nice of her to reward my fear and hurt.

My mother loved watching me crumble. Often it was all that saved me from something worse, so I accepted it for what it was. Her treatment always made me feel dull and as though a part of my essential spark dimmed out of existence. Sometimes, it felt like she was killing me by taking bits of my soul. Little by little she erased me away; extinguishing the light of my soul.

Forget slavery, parenting is where the power is. This is one area in which the "Golden Rule" of treating people the way you wanted to be treated reign's king. I mean, no one wants to interfere with another person's parenting because they don't want anyone interfering with theirs. Everyone uses the excuse that "it's not their business" and they look the other way; "don't ask, don't tell" and all that crap. I guess the old adage is true, "ignorance is bliss."

So there I stood, knowing I was utterly powerless and entirely alone. There'd be no Calvary to ride in and save me from this dictator. Even those who knew what was happening behind closed doors kept quiet; no one challenged mother. I was destined to suffer until one of us grew weary enough to end the game.

I would have liked to have ended the game then and there. I briefly considered my chances. I tried to estimate how much damage I could inflict on my mother before my step-dad reached us. That was a little too tantalizing for my taste, so I quickly turned my thoughts elsewhere. A dark shadow passed by, sending a cold chill up my spine.

As I cleaned, my mother sat back and enjoyed the beer my step-dad presented to her. She looked very smug, especially when my step-dad threw me a disgusted look before returning to the kitchen. When the phone rang, my mother answered as though nothing were upsetting her. She was sugary sweet and laughed easily with her friend, chatting like she was nothing but content. I rolled my eyes when she wasn't looking and I had my back to her.

Every now and then she'd ask her friend to hold the line so she could address me. Mom would cover the phone and intensely growl quiet orders or instructions at me. Though she was engaged in her conversation, she remained vigilant in her observation of me. She was quick to call me on my errors and she never missed anything I did. She was especially vocal about the things she wanted done, but I hadn't accomplished.

At one point, she barked at me to do something, but I neglected to move fast enough in response. It didn't matter that she'd told me to do a dozen things at once and I wasn't sure what to do first. In that moment, she threatened to hit me with the phone. I ducked and ran to attend the task she had demanded last; obviously that was the priority in the list of orders. She kicked me hard, knocking me off my feet as I passed her, but I quickly scrambled back up and raced to obey her.

Casually, my mother returned to her phone call. She apologized to her friend and acted annoyed about having an ungrateful daughter. She continued to joke with her friend as she complained about my many faults. It was obvious that her friend was egging her on and bitching about her own kids as well. They seemed to be having a great time at our expense and humiliation.

***

When I woke, I was a bit disoriented. I knew I wasn't at home, but it took me a minute to realize that I was still in the hospital. I could hear people scuffling around out in the hallway and voices murmuring in quiet conversation. There was anticipation in the air, so I knew something was afoot.

Just then, the nurse, Carol, popped her head into my room after giving the door a gentle knock. The door hadn't been latched shut; it had sat ajar about a foot, so it was not a big deal whether Carol knocked or not. At least, it made no difference to me. I appreciated the courteous gesture none-the-less.

Carol smiled kindly at me and asked, "How are you doing, sweetie?"

I yawned and stretched deeply. My whole body hurt and my arm was aching with a hot throbbing, but I felt more coherent. I wiped the sleep from my eyes and pushed the hair out of my face before answering calmly, "Good. Thank you."

I remembered Carol from a foggy memory; she'd been one of the nurses who had admitted me to the ward. I had liked her when I first saw her and I liked her still. She was a beautiful woman who felt familiar due to her resemblance to Beyoncé. She was definitely a woman of mixed heritage, her skin a perfect caramel color with a flawless complexion. The golden hue to her thick dark hair gave it a light appearance that was very becoming in conjunction with her skin.

I always loved mixed-race children; I thought they were the most beautiful kids in the world. Not only were they beautiful collaborations of different heritages, but they were proof that love can transcend all obstacles; beauty could exist instead of hate. That inspired me and gave me hope in the nature of people; we had the ability to move beyond who we were. We didn't have to live in a world of hate and these children were living examples of the good our togetherness could reap.

"Supper is being served in the day room," Carol informed me.

"I'm not really hungry," I told her shyly. I liked her and I was afraid to offend or anger her by potentially telling her something she didn't like. However, I was nervous of leaving my room and honestly, I wasn't hungry.

"It's okay," she told me, sensing my discomfort. "Everyone needs to come to supper. Try to eat what you can and even if you can't eat anything, it is okay, but you need to attend. We just want to have everyone out of their rooms and socializing a bit."

"Okay," I replied and obediently walked towards the door. I was used to ignoring my own impulses and complying with the demands of others.

Carol smiled warmly at me and placed her hand on my back between my shoulder blades when I approached her. She guided me gently through the door with the hand on my back and pointed in the correct direction with her other hand. I eyed her nervously, but started off in the direction she pointed.

"You're not coming with me?" I inquired softly.

"Not yet," Carol smiled encouragingly. "I have to get a few other people and then I'll see you down there."

"Okay," I said with uncertainty. I was reluctant to leave the security of her presence, but I did.

As I walked down the hallway, I tried to avoid eye contact with the people around me. I felt no judgment about the other patients, but I was embarrassed being there. My presence in the mental ward was an accident. Sooner or later someone would realize the mistake that had been made and they'd let me go. After all, I wasn't really crazy, irrational, delusional, or overly emotional, was I?

I wasn't really sure how I had gotten here; most of the day leading up to my arrival on the floor was hazy and unreal. I remembered crying, but who wouldn't cry if they'd been stabbed? Wouldn't you be crazy if you *didn't* cry? I remembered feeling like I was no longer in control of my body to some extent because I hadn't been able to stop crying when I wanted to and I wasn't able to focus well on anything. Still, that made sense considering the situation.

Maybe I couldn't get a clear version of events in my head, but that didn't make me crazy. I mean, I'm not crazy. Yet, here I was locked in a mental ward and I had no comprehension of how I ended up there. The whole situation was perplexing to me.

I stopped a little way down the hallway and looked back at Carol. She had just come back out of another patient's room. When she realized I was looking at her, she smiled at me in a friendly, though inquisitive manner. I worked my way back over to her and decided to pluck up the courage to ask her the things I wanted to know; I needed to know.

"Where are the police?" I asked Carol quietly.

"What?" Carol seemed surprised by my question.

"The police," I tried again after clearing my throat. "Where are they? Shouldn't they be here since I was attacked?"

The nurse gave me a weary look and I immediately felt afraid. When she didn't respond, I tried a new tactic. I wanted to work up to my main question of "Why am I here?" and not just blurt it out straight away.

"Where's my mother?" I asked. "Do the police have her?"

"What?" Carol asked me again. This time she continued talking, saying, "Sweetie, why would the police have your mom?"

"Because she tried to kill me," I said simply.

Carol, the nurse, stopped in the middle of the hallway. "Is that what you think happened, honey?"

"Yes," I told her. "That is what I think happened because that *is* what happened."

"Oh, sweetie," she said, in such a sad voice. Carol wrapped her right arm around my shoulder and took my left hand in hers. By her encouragement, we resumed walking towards the day room side by side, her still holding onto me. When we reached the day room entrance, she took a tray out of the metal cart wheeled up from the kitchen and handed it to me.

As she pointed to the doorway, Carol instructed me to, "Go sit down wherever you feel comfortable and try to have a little something to eat. When you're done, turn your tray in there so one of the nurses can assess how much you've eaten, if anything."

I gave her a look of concern, worried about what they were assessing exactly. Why were they keeping track of my meals and would they get mad at me if I didn't eat anything? I had told Carol straight up that I wasn't hungry. Was I going to get in trouble?

Carol smiled warmly and tried to ease my concerns by saying, "we don't like to waste any food here. If we can salvage items for the evening snack, we'll remove them from the trays before returning them to the kitchen."

Her explanation made me feel better. I didn't want to waste food either, hence the reason why I'd told her I wasn't hungry. I worried that once I took possession of the tray then no one else would want it. Of course, I understood each patient received a meal, but still, if I wasn't hungry, I didn't need one at all; they could just write that down. Then someone else could be given my allotment; a hungry staff member even.

Carol noted that I had visibly relaxed so she added, "When you've finished, go ahead and return to your room. The doctor will be here shortly after dinner to meet with you."

I took the tray with a tentative smile. I turned to the doorway that led to the day room. It was filled with tables and chairs, most of which were occupied by people in various colors of hospital-issued pajamas; scrubs of sorts. As expected, everyone looked at me as I entered the room. I felt like a spectacle and I wanted to shrink under their attentive stares.

There was a television on and the evening news was playing. People were talking to one another and debating whether to keep the news on or turn the station to *Wheel of Fortune*. I preferred the serenity of my private room, but since I had to be here, I'd have liked *Wheel of Fortune*. The news was so depressing in and of itself, though I didn't bother to add my input.

I hated the news and avoided it like the plague. I couldn't watch it without getting emotional; either I'd be so angry I would be yelling at the television or I'd be so sad, I would cry. Of course, I couldn't imagine either reaction helping me out of this situation. Instead, I opted to ignore the television completely and to keep my eyes averted as much as possible. I walked silently to the table with the fewest people, where they seemed the least likely to start a conversation with me.

People watched me as I took my seat and some smiled at me in silent greeting. I wasn't comfortable with any of the interactions, but I wasn't going to be rude. I tried to smile back, but I felt awkward and exposed. I quickly took my place at the table and tried to blend in, hoping to be forgotten. Thankfully, people seemed to lose interest in me as they turned their attention back to their evening meals.

The people at my table greeted me kindly, but seemed to understand my aloofness. I was relieved to find them respectful of my desire to avoid conversation. They chatted easily amongst themselves, trading food and giggling about it since they knew that was against the rules. It was obvious they'd been here a while and knew each other somewhat, at least enough to converse casually.

It didn't take long for the room to return to its previous state or for new arrivals to draw the occupants' attention. I was able to sit relatively unnoticed, avoiding eye contact, and staying intensely focused on the tray in front of me. I fumbled with the individually wrapped items that were laid out in an organized fashion before me, but I didn't eat.

The well-portioned and balanced meal consisted of a small piece of chicken breast, green beans, and mashed potatoes. There was a slice of bread on the side and a small container of yellow Jell-O. There was also a fresh orange on my tray, along with a small carton of milk and a covered mug that contained some sort of broth. I liked the food they offered me, but I simply had no appetite.

Lost in my own thoughts, I finally ventured a look around. For the first time since my arrival, I checked out my surroundings in detail. The day room was just off the main hallway by the nurses' station and the secured entry point for the unit. It was painted light blue and had a linoleum floor that sported blue and red lines that created a geometric pattern. It had been waxed to a shine, as most hospital floors are and I was impressed with its level of cleanliness.

The room I'd initially been brought to for my intake evaluation hadn't impressed me. I felt like the small reception room should have been cleaner, if not more colorful. I dismissed my misgivings, assuming the small room had been more for storage or something since my assigned room was so tidy. Seeing the well-groomed day room made me feel more satisfied with the ability of the cleaning crew, the level of sanitary expectations, and the hospitals overall presentation.

There were a few places to sit just outside of the nurses' station along the hallway which then stretched out to allow for the various rooms along the L-shaped hall. At the other end of the hall was another area that had a smaller day room. There was also another nurses' station, again smaller than the one by the entrance to the unit. These smaller rooms lay in a locked corridor within the unit and I noted additional rooms there as well. It appeared that there was additional staff there, serving dinner to the few occupants that stayed in that section.

I realized they must be the higher-risk patients, for whatever reason. I was happy that I wasn't in the more secure section, though I envied the low population that resided there. That aspect would have been lovely at least. I didn't feel very comfortable in crowds, especially in a crowd of unpredictable people. The group I currently found myself with certainly fit the bill of erratically behaved people.

I still hadn't figured out why I was there, considering that I had been the one attacked. Shouldn't I be in a normal hospital unit or rather, shouldn't I have been released after receiving my initial care? I hoped the doctor coming to speak to me would clear matters up. It was obvious none of the nursing staff planned to do anything. They were nice enough, but none of them seemed to want to give me any useful information.

Feeling irritated, I turned my attention back to my meal again. I liked how the bread was in its own little plastic sleeve thing. I always liked those cute little pats of butter from the cafeteria. The napkin was wrapped up with the salt and pepper inside another little plastic sleeve that included the plastic eating utensils.

The "silverware" was made entirely of plastic, like we were having a picnic or something. They were also colored in a deep shade of orange with dull edges. I assumed this was meant to prevent someone from using them to hurt themselves or anyone else. I assumed the color was to enable the staff to see and identify the plastic-ware more easily. I found that to be weird.

That was the point at which I finally had enough. I hurriedly drank my carton of milk so I could say I consumed something then I rose to take my tray to the front. As I prepared to go, a burly man asked me if he could have my bread and I nodded my consent. This prompted another man to inquire if he could have my yellow Jell-O. Again, I nodded consent as I held my tray out towards them.

As soon as I could, I migrated toward the door to turn in my tray. I didn't bother to explain that I hadn't eaten the missing items, not that anyone cared to ask. I just remained quiet so I could return to my room without further delay. I was relieved to make my way down the corridor and to slip into the solitude of my private domain.

CHAPTER FIVE

I felt a twinge of surprise as the tip of my mother's steak knife pricked me in the elbow. I moved fast enough, removing my elbow from the table, to avoid any real damage. The mark she left was no worse than when the dog scratched me before its claws were trimmed.

"Keep your fucking elbows off the table," my mother ordered through gritted teeth.

My mother was trying to keep her anger in check. She and my step-dad had plans and they were expecting friends over shortly after dinner. I knew that I'd have to be quick about cleaning up. My mother wouldn't tolerate any messes when their guests arrived.

I wasn't happy about my parents' plans. They'd invited my step-dad's best friend, Bill, along with two other couples they frequently hung out with, Tom and Silvia Baines and Molly Sims with her girlfriend, Alice. I wasn't really sure what made these people enjoy time with my parents, but I knew what my parents liked about them.

Tom and Silvia were very active in the neighborhood committees. They held a lot of clout when it came to the people in our area and it didn't hurt that they were wealthy to boot. My mother loved power; she was drawn to it like fish to water. She felt that she gained esteem by interacting with Tom and Silvia. She went out of her way to cater to them and to charm them. I thought my mother appeared pathetically fake and needy, but the Baines' seemed to enjoy having their egos constantly stroked by her. Perhaps they were just as fake and needy as she was?

My mother was very proud to be friends with Molly and Alice; she thought she was a progressive, modern woman by having lesbian friends. She believed her association with them made her a good person since she was showing great charity by accepting their lifestyle. In truth, I wondered if she wasn't really a lesbian herself, and just too concerned with public opinion to be who she really was. That'd explain a lot actually, especially since she never seemed to have any sort of intimacy with my step-dad. Maybe he liked her because she let him sleep around? As long as no one was the wiser and he left her alone, she didn't seem to care what he did.

Bill had been best friends with my step-dad since they were children. They grew up next door to one another and had been more like brothers. Neither of them had any siblings of their own, so that bound them tighter. My step-dad was horribly co-dependent and that had been to Bill's benefit until my mother entered the picture.

My mother didn't actually like Bill, but she tolerated him for my step-dad's sake. Of course, his large bank account and his propensity to shower my mother in gifts didn't hurt either. I was convinced my mother only allowed the relationship because Bill offered a distraction when my step-dad became overbearing. Though my mom loved having a loyal lackey, she needed breaks now and then from his obsessive adoration. Bill gave her that.

Bill didn't seem to like my mother any more than she liked him, but he had his own reasons for maintaining the relationship. I knew Bill enjoyed gallivanting around town, sharing the company of whores in the seedy end of town. My step-dad would follow him blindly into any situation and would support Bill in every endeavor. Bill enjoyed the undying allegiance of my step-dad, so he seemed content to pay tribute to my mother in order to have his trashy cohort.

Bill was the only one who lived some distance away from us and I knew that meant he'd stay the night. He liked to drink and though we didn't usually have alcohol in our house, my mother made an exception for Bill. She never bought his liquor, but she always allowed him to bring whatever booze he wanted without complaint. My parents even kept a small refrigerator on hand for him to stock his poison in during his visits.

I wasn't accustomed to smelling alcohol since my parents rarely drank and I hated how Bill smelled. My mother never drank when Bill was around though she'd allow my step-dad to have a few drinks, but only when Bill insisted. This was her way of keeping Bill happy and his purse strings loose. I didn't like the scent of alcohol, but worse was the behavior it produced in people, especially when they drank as much as Bill did.

I really hated how creepy Bill was and how he looked at me. The more he drank, the more obvious his interest was and the more direct his comments. He was an odd one when he was sober, but at least he managed his behavior then. When he'd had something to drink, all bets were off and he lacked any filters.

My mother didn't mind Bill's drinking. The more intoxicated he got, the more he gave her. I was sure he had no idea what he gave her, but she'd acquire inside stock information and trading tips for free. She'd also coerce monetary gifts more easily from him. Apparently they all lacked scruples.

Bill was always trying to coax me into drinking with him which always made my parents laugh. My mother would usually throw in some snide remark about how I only drank with "my skanky friends" or how I'd "jump on his offer like flies on shit" if my parents weren't there to supervise me. This was usually followed up with a round of insults and more laughter, all at my expense. It was always fun when Bill came to stay; I couldn't wait for his visits. Yay! I sighed deeply.

Thinking about the pending night, I rolled my eyes without thinking. Unfortunately, my mother hadn't missed my expression. She quickly sprang on me, taking the opportunity to attack. I should've known better than to leave myself so unguarded. Mother always looked for a reason to toss me out of the house when company came.

This mother's inclination to expel me from the house served several purposes. First, it gave my mother something to bitch about which was always a favorite of hers. Second, it made her look like a caring mother struggling to raise a wild child and that reaped undeserved support from her guests. Lastly, it gave her a reason to expel me from being around her entertaining night of fun. The last reason gave her the freedom to relax and enjoy herself without potential interruptions from me.

"Did you roll your eyes at me?" she demanded.

"No, I - ," she stopped me in mid-sentence by slapping me across the face.

"Don't lie to me, you hussy," she screamed. "I saw you, you ungrateful wretch."

I didn't bother to say anything else. I sat there, holding my mouth and looking down. I spoke only when I was spoken to and only with the appropriate responses my mother expected. I knew she'd blow through her routine quickly as long as I didn't agitate the situation. She'd want things handled before her friends arrived, so I played the game with her in an effort to navigate the ritual faster.

My mother looked at my half-eaten plate. I knew she was contemplating how long it would take me to finish my meal. The grim look she gave me told me that she figured it would take longer than she was willing to wait. That didn't bode well for me.

"You're done eating," she told me. "You'll save that plate for your meal tomorrow. Now get the dishes done and get out."

"Get out?" I questioned, surprised and unsure. I had assumed she'd simply relegate me to my bedroom, not banish me from the house.

"Yes," she smiled at me wickedly, happy to see my reaction, "get out."

"Of the house," I unwisely asked for verification.

"What the hell is wrong with you?" my mother demanded to know. "Yes, out of the house."

"Where am I meant to go?" I asked though I was afraid of setting her off again.

"I really don't give a fuck," she snapped. "You can't seem to care enough about me to do the simple things I ask, so why should I care? I wash my hands of you; I'm done."

"Good riddance," my step-dad offered in support.

"But you're my mom!" I looked at her confused. Though I'd love to get away from my mother, I had nowhere to go and I was under the legal age to be on my own.

"Don't remind me," she scowled as she stood up. I had a moment of panic until she added, "However, being your mother, I'm legally obligated to give you what you need until you're eighteen. Taking that into account, I'll graciously allow your sorry ass to stay in the loft of the garage."

I felt deep relief, "Thank you, mom."

"You don't deserve it, but I'm too good a person to let you stay on the streets," she replied. Then she pointed in my face with her index finger in warning, "But if you need to use the bathroom, you'd better use the gas station down the block because you're not coming back into my house – at least not until you learn some respect!"

With that, my mother dismissed me from the table. She and my step-dad busied themselves with excited preparation for the coming evening while I tackled the messy kitchen. I was part way through the dishes when the guests began arriving. Though I had worked fast and diligently, it hadn't been enough effort. My mother wasn't pleased with my continued presence any more than I was at still being on hand.

Bill came in just behind Molly and Alice. My mother was delighted as she greeted them. She wasted no time in telling them about my fabled indiscretions and how she was forced to punish me. She explained that since I didn't know how to behave in a house, I'd be staying in the garage like the uncivilized animal that I was. Of course, her friends backed her up and encouraged her.

Everyone seemed to have an opinion about me, my upbringing, and my lack of respect. Everyone cheered my mother, saying what a great mom she was. Apparently, they all agreed that it was a privilege to live in a house, not a right. Since I lacked understanding of this, it was an important lesson for me to learn.

"I don't know how you do it," Alice said, eyeing me in disappointment.

"Well, it's difficult, but sometimes you have to love them enough to say no," my mother informed her childless friends.

"I don't think I could do it," Bill said. "I'd probably end up in jail for beating her."

My mother chuckled, "Well, she's in the hospital enough with her self-inflicted injuries. I can't imagine anyone would notice if I did beat her."

"As if you ever would, darling," my step-dad chimed in right on cue. Looking at each of their friends, he added, "She loves her too much; that's why she pampers Tiffany more than she should."

"Oh, sweetheart," my mother replied, feigning embarrassment while he winked at her.

"Tiffany should be thankful she has a loving, involved mother like you," Molly said. "You're always there for her and you provide her with a lovely home."

"Thank you," my mother responded, choking up as though she were so overcome with emotion it was hard to speak. "You're *too* kind."

"We're just speaking the truth," Alice commented.

I kept quiet and worked to complete my tasks faster. I just wanted to be away from these people. Of course, they all chimed in to rehash the story when Tom and Silva arrived. Amazingly enough, my behavior had grown more hideous than it'd been in the first rendition of the story. Each time the tale was told, I grew less appealing as a person and my mother grew more dramatic in her portrayal of me.

Tom and Silvia were naturally aghast and thought I deserved to be tossed out of the house as well. Silvia even said how she "wouldn't trust me in her house," saying it so I'd hear her loud and clear. They were a bunch of assholes, all of them.

When I finished my chores and headed to my room, my mother hollered at me to stop where I was. "Where do you think you're going?" she demanded to know.

"I was going to grab some pajamas and get my pillow," I answered.

"I don't think so, young lady," my mother said as though she were insulted. "Legally, I only have to provide you with what's necessary; shelter, food, and clothing."

I looked at the other people in the room for help. If nothing else, didn't pajamas constitute as clothing? Shouldn't I at least be allowed that? Was no one going to call my mother out on her craziness?

In a weak, uncertain voice I asked, "Aren't pajamas clothes?" My mother's eyes nearly glowed from the heat of her anger.

"You have a full belly, you're wearing nice clothes, and you have a place to stay in the garage. I don't need to do anymore," my mother said as though I'd asked her for a human sacrifice, not simply pajamas and a pillow.

I looked around the room once again. My step-dad refused to look at me, focusing intently on my mother; nothing new there. Tom and Silvia tried to act like nothing was happening and disengaged from the interaction. Molly was nodding in agreement with my mother and Alice patted my mother supportively on the shoulder.

"Maybe you'll learn to appreciate the things your parents do for you," Molly told me.

"She doesn't care," my mother dramatically burst into fake tears. "We work so hard to give her everything and she just spits in our faces."

"Oh, don't cry, dear," my step-dad cooed, taking my mother into his arms. "Look what you did to your mother!"

"How could you be so selfish?" Alice asked.

"Just get out!" my mother bellowed.

I wasted no time in exiting the house and scrambling into the garage loft. I couldn't get away from those people fast enough. I didn't care where I'd be sleeping; I was just happy to escape. My heart was beating rapidly, I felt hot, and nothing seemed real. My chest ached from the tightness that spread through it and I struggled to restrain my tears. I just needed a few minutes to pull myself together.

The loft was cluttered with storage items packed in various boxes. Thankfully, my parents' old mattress was still stored up there; it'd do nicely for a bed. The mattress smelled dusty, but at least it was in a safe, sheltered place. There weren't any linens to speak of and it we devoid of pillows, but I wouldn't have to sleep directly on the floor. That was something, especially since the nights were growing colder as winter approached.

I sat quietly for a long while, trying to steady my breathing. I took the opportunity to dream about all the possibilities life held in store for me. I fantasized about the day I'd get to leave this place and really begin my life. It was a comfort and I enjoyed the serenity of the moment.

The light in the loft was weak and dingy so I just left it off. There was a full moon so I could see well enough because of the light coming through the double windows that overlooked the driveway below. I found the loft to be a calming place and not the punishment my mother had intended it to be. I was grateful for that and after a while of singing softly to myself, I decided to lie down.

The loft proved to be better insulated than I thought it was. It rarely got down to freezing in our part of Texas, but I sure was glad the storage boxes and junk helped to maintain the temperature. The little space I had was warmed easily by my body heat, so I felt fairly comfortable. I was happy that I didn't need a blanket after all, though I would have loved a pillow.

I was wearing a pair of jogging pants with a sweatshirt over a tank top. I had pulled my bra off and laid it next to the mattress with my shoes in an effort to get more comfortable, but I felt too warm to remain in the sweatshirt. I pulled the sweatshirt off over my head. I thought it'd make a nice pillow, so I wadded it up and bunched it under my head. It wasn't long before I started to dose off.

I wasn't sure what time it was when I heard him approaching. The moon had moved out of the way of the windows, so the light pouring in was much fainter than it'd been earlier. This meant that it must be sometime after midnight, I figured. I could tell by the ruckus he was making that Bill had enjoyed a large amount of alcohol. This put me on full alert and I held my breath, hoping he'd just go back out the way he'd come in.

When he started to climb the ladder to the loft, my heart began beating faster. Fear surged through me and I quickly retreated into the darker corners, hoping he wouldn't notice me. I hoped Bill would think I had gone somewhere else for the night or lose interest when he found me missing. Maybe he'd lose his footing and fall off the ladder or landing, discouraging him and forcing him away before he got too close.

"I know you're here, Tiff-Tiff," he giggled. "Don't play coy with me, you little vixen."

Bill was wobbling a bit as he pulled himself from the ladder to a standing position. Even from where I was hiding I could smell the booze permeating from him. I wanted to vomit. I covered my mouth hoping to mask any sounds I might make, breathing or otherwise.

"Come out, come out wherever you are," Bill said in a voice that made me shiver.

When I didn't move or make a sound, Bill began to get angry. He started ranting to himself about how my mother was right; I *was* an ungrateful, stupid bitch. He started to tell me how he planned to teach me a thing or two when he found me and that the longer I made him wait, the worse my lesson would be. I started to shake uncontrollably and accidently bumped into a box, exposing my location.

I shrieked as he dove at me. I was surprised by his speed and strength despite his alcohol level. It certainly didn't help matters that I was sort of trapped in a corner by clutter. My hopes of escape were completely shattered.

"There you are, you whore," Bill said with an excitement that curdled my blood. "Your mother told me about you, you filthy, filthy slut and now you get to show your ole Uncle Bill just how you like it."

"Get away from me," I screamed, kicking at him as hard as I could. I screamed incoherently when he grasped my one of my legs tightly. I thrashed about trying to break free from his hold.

"Stop fighting or I'll have to strike you," Bill threatened.

"Screw you!" I screamed as I bucked wildly.

"Yeah, you will," Bill laughed menacingly and then punched me hard in the gut.

The blow to my stomach made my breath *whoosh* from my body. I stopped bucking and tried to curl into a ball, reaching to hold my belly. I was unable to move in the way I intended. Instead, I found Bill making his way up my body, between my legs. His heavy body pinned me down easily. I was struggling to breathe, let alone put up a fight.

Bill grabbed my jaw with his hand and licked the side of my face. I tried to turn my head back and forth to stop him, but his grip was rock hard. It hurt and I knew with certainty that there'd be bruises on my face come morning. I realized that would probably be the least of my concerns once Bill had finished with me.

"Fight all you want, slutty little tramp," he told me. "No one can hear you out here and I find the challenge inviting. See for yourself," he said as he moved my hand to his crotch.

To my surprise, Bill had already removed his pants. The racket he'd made when he first came into the garage must have been caused by his disrobing. His erect penis was hard against my hand, so I grasped it tightly, exciting Bill. When I started to pull as hard as I could, Bill yelped, realizing my true intention; I was going to pull the member from his body.

When the pain penetrated his alcohol clouded brain, he yelled, "Bitch!" Then he punched me in the gut again. I immediately released him in order to protect my abdomen.

"I want to leave my mark on you so badly, but I'll be careful," he sneered as he tenderly traced my jawline. "Though I want to leave you with something to remember me by, I don't want to alarm anyone by ruining that beautiful face of yours."

I snapped at him, trying to bite him. He was repugnant and I was repulsed by his touch. Bill just laughed at my attempts to fight; he was so much stronger than me that we both knew I didn't stand a chance against him. He grabbed my chin in his hand and kissed me in a sloppy, open-mouthed way that left me spitting. Then, in one smooth motion that seemed to be well practiced, he tore my jogging pants down and slammed inside me.

I felt gut-wrenching pain that made me scream in agony. I was a virgin and I wasn't prepared for this by any stretch of the imagination. It felt like my insides were tearing, but I couldn't shove Bill off me and I couldn't figure out any other way to stop the pain. I was at a complete loss. My brain was muddled by fear, pain, and panic.

Bill complained about the dry state of my tender opening. As a solution, he grabbed the flask of booze he'd brought with him in his jacket pocket and poured the contents on us both. I don't know if it helped him or not, but it made me scream again. The alcohol burnt the damaged skin of my sensitive vagina; it was as if he had poured flames directly on to my nether region.

"That's right, baby," he spoke like we were lovers and my screams were in ecstasy instead of pain. "Let me hear you."

He continued to hump me like a horny dog as I prayed for the end. With all the jokes I'd heard about men not lasting long in the sack, I was confused and frustrated by his longevity. It slowly dawned on me that he wasn't reaching orgasm quickly because of his level of intoxication. This became apparent to me as he started to complain about it. He began talking to his penis in hopes of coaxing it to ejaculate.

Bill continued to hold my body down with his body weight and by using me as a brace to maintain the position he wanted. He used me to help stabilize his position and to cushion himself from the abrasive floor we were laying on. On his haste to conquer me, he ignored the mattress and just forced himself upon me right where he'd knocked me down.

I was pinned tightly, but I could feel the gritty wood of the loft tearing at my exposed back and buttocks. Fighting to push Bill off of me and struggling to break free from his capture only seemed to worsen the damage the floor was causing to my skin. I focused on that sensation in the hope of detaching myself from the other pains Bill was causing my body.

"There we go! There we go!" he exclaimed and I knew he was finally reaching the climax he needed to end this nightmare.

Just as he started to orgasm, Bill slammed himself as deep as he could into me. When he was fully satiated, he collapsed on top of me, allowing his full weight to crush against me. As he came completely down on top of me, the pressure knocked the wind out of me and the arm that had been helping to support his weight slammed across my neck. This pushed my head at an upward angle and cut off my air.

Struggling to breath, I sputtered a bit as I was being choked. Bill thought my jerking around was due to his ability to make me orgasm along with him. I heard Bill mumbling something that sounded like he was proud of himself, but I couldn't hold onto any of the words. I couldn't comprehend what he was saying and I blacked out before he crawled off me.

***

Walking back to my room, I pondered the orange plastic eating utensils. They seemed weird to me. Were they really meant to stop a person from trying to use them as an instrument for harm? If they were, I thought it was a poor effort and ineffective overall.

I started to think of the various ways a person could use the utensils in order to cause damage. My first thought was the obvious one – even a blunt object could penetrate the skin or a vulnerable orifice if enough force was applied. Granted, the plastic-ware might break, but that would just leave a sharper edge. Then I considered the slight serration of the knife. Yeah, I could inflict pain with it. It was silly to think I couldn't.

I started to think about all the things that the staff had in place in order to keep the patients safe. I understood the reasons they did what they did and I was sure the hospital knew that no one truly determined would be completely thwarted. Still, all efforts to mitigate a potential situation had been made. The chances of an incident occurring had been greatly reduced.

Nevertheless, the tools were there if one wanted to use them. Though bath soaps were given out in single shower portions and tracked by the supply closet nurse, what would stop a person from drinking the soap? I thought perhaps the hospital had thought of that. They most likely used a non-toxic cleanser, but still, I'd think it would at least make a person ill, right?

No one was allowed to use deodorant; the alternative was baby powder. If you needed to shave, a nurse had to do the actual shaving. A patient in the mental ward was never left alone or given sole use of such a thing as a razor. I had to acknowledge and even applauded the efforts put forth for safety, but "where there's a will, there's a way" is a popular expression for a reason.

I made my way back to my room and quietly sat on the side of the bed. I continued to think of ways a person could harm themselves or someone else despite the precautions taken. They could simply drown themselves in the toilet water or bash their heads against a hard surface. If someone were determined enough, these small steps would do little to prevent them from their goal. If someone wanted to die, they'd find a way.

Just then, I noticed the doctor standing in my doorway, asking me if I was okay. Pulling me from my reveries was a tiny woman of Asian descent with a distinct American accent. She had hypnotizing almond eyes and sleek short black hair. She didn't look old enough to be a physician, but indeed she was.

"I'm fine. Thank you," I replied quietly, though cordially. "I was just thinking."

She nodded at me thoughtfully then said, "Well, I'm Dr. Triton and I was hoping we could talk for a while."

"Okay," I said numbly. I didn't really feel like talking, but I didn't reckon I really had a choice in the matter either.

The doctor came in and took a seat in the hard plastic chair. It didn't escape my notice that the chair was positioned so it sat between the exit and me. No doubt, this was another security measure; one that offered a safe retreat in case a patient flipped out on the healthcare provider. Since I'd been the one attacked and not the one who actually committed the assault, I found this to be odd behavior. Still, I dismissed it easily, accepting it as standard practice in this profession and setting.

Dr. Triton watched me for a few minutes before asking, "Tiffany, do you know where you are?"

"Yes," I answered, trying not to show my irritation. "I'm in a hospital. Have the police been called yet?"

"Why would we call the police, Tiffany?" the doctor looked perplexed. "Do you think we should call them because you're here?"

Ugh. This was great; I got the stupid kid on the block. "No, I don't think you should call the police because I'm here."

"Then why do you think the police should be called?" Dr. Triton leaned forward, shifting her weight to her elbows as they rested on her knees.

"You should call them because of *why* I'm here." I was really unimpressed with this doctor and hoped the rest of the doctors on staff were better. I bet this was one of those student residents. Yeah, that was my luck.

Dr. Triton looked deeply interested. "And why do you think you ended up here?"

"I'm here because someone tried to kill me," I said calmly. "Usually when a person is attacked, the police are notified."

"You were attacked?" Dr. Triton looked a little confused. She checked her notes to see whether she'd overlooked something in my chart.

"Yes, someone tried to kill me."

Dr. Triton looked up from the chart and re-inspected me carefully. After a few minutes, she asked me, "Tiffany, do you know *who* tried to kill you?"

"Yes," I told her, curious about what the chart said since she hadn't seemed to know I'd been attacked. "My mother; my mother tried to kill me."

"Tiffany, it says here that your mother was the one who found you and brought you to the emergency room."

"She brought me to the emergency room, but not because she *found* me," I explained. I raised my left arm up and added, "My mother did this to me."

"Why would she do that?" Dr. Triton asked me. "Why do you believe your mother would intentionally harm you and then bring you to the emergency room?"

"My mother hates me," I said coldly. "She resents me and she enjoys hurting me. I think she got angry enough this time that she actually wanted to kill me, but when she saw all the blood I was losing, she got scared. She didn't want to be prosecuted for my murder. After all, what would the neighbors think?"

"Tiffany, I'm only concerned with what you think," Dr. Triton said, dismissing my private attack on my mother's persona. "Do you really believe your mother did this to you?"

"Yes," I replied angrily. Hadn't I just told the doctor what had happened?

"Tiffany," Dr. Triton said in a very low and careful voice. She leaned in towards me as though she was trying to soften the information she was trying to relay. I realized she was trying to be tender as she gingerly explained things to me. "Your mother didn't do this to you."

"How the hell do you know?" I demanded and why did she keep repeating my name? Who said someone's name that damn much?

"I know because of the ER report."

"What?" I couldn't believe my ears. I knew what happened; I was there. This woman hadn't been there so how could she, or anyone else, validate anything?

"The ER report," she repeated. She must have thought I was questioning what ER was because she added, "ER means emergency room."

"No shit, Sherlock," I snapped. Yeah, she was definitely a student resident; had to be.

Dr. Triton ignored my seething rebuke and kept on with the conversation as though I had never barked at her. "It says you got angry and grabbed the butcher's knife off the counter. According to your mother, you threatened to stab her, but then told her that you'd 'show her' by stabbing yourself instead."

"I did no such thing," I said. I was vaguely aware that the volume of my voice was starting to rise. "*She* stabbed *me*."

"It says that your mother screamed and you just laughed, telling her you'd blame her. She said you told her everyone would believe you because no one would believe you would hurt yourself," Dr. Triton read.

"Of course, I wouldn't hurt myself," I snapped at her. "Do you think I'm crazy?" It dawned on me that she did; she did think I was crazy and that was really why I was here. Fuck.

"Your mother said she was too afraid to call 911 because she didn't know what you'd do; she didn't want to provoke you further. She was worried you'd hurt yourself worse than you already had."

"I didn't hurt myself," I told her through clenched teeth.

"Maybe you just don't remember the incident properly," Dr. Triton tried to convince me. "After all, you did lose a lot of blood."

"Yeah, because my mother stabbed me in the fucking arm," I bellowed. I was not only angry, but frustrated. Why couldn't the doctor see this was a defensive wound?

"Your mother said that you began to calm down after inserting the knife; she figured from the rapid blood loss. That was when she called 911, but she wasn't sure the paramedics would get to you in time so she raced you here."

"Bullshit!" I spat out. "She's *lying* just like she always does."

"Why would she lie?" Dr. Triton asked in a patronizing voice. "If your mother had injured you, why would she have gone through the trouble of calling 911 or bringing you here?"

"Because she's crazy!" I snapped.

"Well, the ER report says that the physician on duty noted you were acting very peculiar and that you were very hostile towards your mother," Dr. Triton read aloud again.

"Of course, I was!" I barked at her. "My mother *tried to kill me*, so obviously I'm going to feel hostile towards her!" I couldn't believe this was happening. Did she really not get it? I thought doctors were supposed to be smart.

Dr. Triton looked at me in a sympathetic way and remarked, "The physician on duty in the ER found no evidence to support your claims. From the angle of the wound, you could have done it yourself."

"Could have, but *didn't*," I said fervently.

"There's no reason for us to think your mother's claims are false. According to the ER report, even the physician on duty believes yours wounds are self-inflicted, not defensive."

"Fuck that damn report, fuck the ER physician on duty, and fuck you too!" I jumped to my feet and apparently frightened the naïve doctor. She quickly jerked away from me and stumbled towards the doorway. "If you believe her then you don't know shit!"

The doctor was calling for additional staff members. Rhonda and a burly black man rushed forward to try to get control of me. I was so angry that I started to cry.

"Don't touch me!" I warned, drawing away from the nurses.

Carol had popped into the room briefly and after some instructions from Dr. Triton, she quickly retreated. I briefly wondered what that was about, but was quickly distracted by the ruckus around me. Dr. Triton was trying to get me to calm down by speaking to me in soothing tones. None of the three made physical contact with my person; they just sort of hovered around me, like they were trying to cage me in with their bodies.

Just then Carol dashed back into the room with something in her hands. This was when Rhonda and the male nurse sprung at me, latching onto me and forcing me to the bed. They pinned me down while Carol injected something into me. I screamed in both shock and rage. Did they really have the right to medicate me without my consent or knowledge?

As the medication took almost immediate effect, I started to feel my body involuntarily relax. The nurses backed away though they stayed ready to apprehend me at a moment's notice. Of course, there was no need for their caution, as I was fading into the darkness that swallowed my consciousness up. The last thing I remember was hearing Dr. Triton apologizing. She was embarrassed because she hadn't handled the situation with more care.

CHAPTER SIX

When I regained consciousness, Bill was gone. I was too exhausted and sore from the ordeal to try to move, so I let sleep consume me. My dreams were vivid and horrifying; my body pulsed and ached adding to the overall effect of the dream. I was too tired to stay awake, but too tormented to truly sleep. I was lost somewhere in between two planes of consciousness and the experience was devastating.

Mercifully, I was alone in the loft, so I allowed myself to cry out my anguish. I was half naked, bleeding and bruised. I was certain I had some slivers in my butt cheeks, but I was alone, and I was alive. That was all I could ask for in the end.

I wondered what my step-dad would think of his "best friend" when he heard what he'd done to me. I pondered the horrible things my mother would do to Bill for raping her daughter. I smiled when I thought about her lashing out at him. For my mother, the fact that this crime was committed on her own property would simply be adding insult to injury.

I shivered in delight at the thought of the cruel things my mother would do. I didn't feel guilty for hoping for the worst of my mother's wrath to rain down on the abhorrent man; he had earned everything she was capable of doling out. Thinking about it made me happy because at least one good thing would come from this nightmare; Bill would get the beating he deserved. My mother would unleash the harm I was too weak to inflict and then banish him from our house.

Since I was only sixteen, I hoped Bill would go to jail. I would love to see him taken away in cuffs by some brutish cops. Oh, how I hoped that I would be allowed to be present when they arrested him. Maybe it was wrong to wish it on him, but I didn't care. The thought made me feel better whether it happened or not. Besides, if I was going to dream then I'd dream big.

As I slowly pulled myself together and made my way to our back door, I fought to retain my composure. The pain was nauseating, but I found strength in knowing the severity of my mother's anger and what it would yield once she discovered what Bill had done. I took refuge in the feeling of pleasure that washed over me; for once, I wouldn't be the recipient of her anger.

When I finally reached the door, it was locked. My parents were sitting just inside at the kitchen table laughing with Bill over coffee. I couldn't wait to knock and end that laughter. I pounded on the door, but it wasn't as forceful as I expected it to be. My energy levels were badly depleted; it had taken a lot out of me to simply get to the house. For a moment, I was afraid they hadn't heard me so I knocked again.

"I'm coming, I'm coming!" my mother bellowed in annoyance.

It was only a few seconds before my mother reached the door and I saw her face. My mother looked ashen and her mouth dropped open with a small gasp. She gripped the door tightly to support herself, alerting my step-dad of trouble.

"Who is it, honey?" he asked my mother.

My mother started to cry, backing up to clear the doorway. At first I thought she had moved so I could get into the house, but then I guessed it was so my step-dad could see me himself. My step-dad rushed forward and embraced my mother, who turned and hid her face in his chest, as though it was too hard to look at me. I couldn't believe how this was affecting my mother. I knew she'd be angry, but seeing her cry made me realize she really did care about me.

"What the fuck?" my step-dad exclaimed in a shocked voice.

I looked directly at Bill and said, "He raped me in the loft last night. He choked me until I blacked out and then he left me for dead."

I was surprised hearing my own ragged voice. I sounded so hateful and angry. My voice didn't resemble any part of what I knew of myself.

"Stop it!" my mother yelled. "Stop it, you fucking whore!"

I couldn't speak. My attention snapped to my mother and I stared at her in disbelief. Was she really trying to say that this was somehow my fault or that I *asked* for this to happen? I looked at Bill and briefly absorbed his wicked smile. He seemed at ease, standing casually as he waited for the show to begin. I started to dry-heave from disgust, understanding that he'd already laid the grounds for his defense.

"How can you come to my door like this, reeking of alcohol? You smell like a sewer," my mother cried like a banshee. "Oh, what will the neighbors think?"

My mother started to move dramatically around the room in a state of panic. I think my step-dad was talking to me, but I couldn't comprehend anything. I was at a complete loss. All I keep seeing was Bill's delight that my mother was angry at me. Wait, what was happening? Was I in the *Twilight Zone*? My step-dad pulled me into the house and closed the door, acting like he was ashamed of me.

"Bill told us all about what you did last night," my mother spat at me, carelessly shoving my step-dad out of the way. "You have a lot of nerve, you tramp!"

"What?" my voice sounded little, even to me.

Bill and my step-dad causally sat back down at the kitchen table and resumed sipping their coffee. I could see them smiling and occasionally I heard them laugh. They were enjoying this tremendously and my mother didn't care. She was blaming me for what Bill had done.

"I can't believe you'd act like a common whore in *my* home," my mother was dripping with hate. "Bill told us how you got drunk then *threw* yourself at him."

"I didn't drink anything," I tried to defend myself.

"I can smell it on you, you stupid bitch," my mother said, pushing me away from her. "You stink like the gutter you belong in."

Again, words eluded me. What the hell was happening here? I heard my step-dad apologizing to Bill for my lack of morals. He was telling him how bad he felt that his stepdaughter was so indecent and he hoped that Bill wouldn't hold them accountable for my bad behavior. It was almost more than I could take.

"Whore!" my mother screamed as she hit me across my face.

My step-dad got up from the table to stand beside my mother. He was trying to offer her support in her moment of horror. He looked at me and bellowed, "Look what you're doing to your mother!"

"You filthy wench," my mother cried in a weaker voice, leaning against my step-dad like she was about to faint from distress. "I don't know who you are anymore. It's bad enough that I worry about what kind of diseases you might be bringing home due to your nasty habits and lack of morals, but now you risk the health of our friend – your father's *best* friend - by *seducing* him."

"What?" I could barely hear my own voice. It sounded like there was a freight train heading towards me at a very rapid speed. The sound was growing louder in my head and my ears rang.

"I can't blame him," my mother said sadly. She looked at Bill, placed her hand gently on his shoulder and added, "I don't blame you. I know it's hard for a man to say no when he's being rubbed on by a naked whore, especially when he's had a drink or two."

"A drink or two," I snorted. A drink or two my ass; Bill had a drink or two for breakfast.

My mother turned her rage back at me in full force, "I can't believe you'd do this to us after all we've done for you. I can't even look at you!"

My mother buried her face in my step-dad's chest again. I stumbled a bit as though I'd been physically struck and I thought I was going to fall. I couldn't believe how wrong this all was and as I stood there in my condition, I couldn't believe my mother couldn't see the truth. Worse yet, I knew somewhere in the back of my mind that she could see the truth, but chose not to; I meant less to her than Bill did – and she disliked him.

"Get her out of here," my mother demanded and finally slumped into my step-dad's arms.

"You heard her, *get out*," my step-dad ordered.

"Wh-where am I supposed to go?" I asked in a shaky voice.

"No one fucking cares," my mother screamed over her shoulder. "Live on the streets where you belong, you trash!"

I turned and walked away, feeling numb and disoriented. When I made my way down the porch stairs, I turned in time to see Bill and my mother consoling each other as my step-dad closed the door on me. I was speechless and stunned; I literally felt stupid. Had this really happened or was I still lost in one of the unimaginable dreams that had plagued me?

I turned from the house in time to see my neighbor's staring at me. I could only imagine what they thought after all the

stories they'd been told by my mother. I wondered how she'd
spin this one; she'd have a lot of damage control ahead of her.

I just turned and walked aimlessly away.

***

As the sedative wore off and I started to regain awareness
of my surroundings, I realized I was limited in the amount of
movement I had. It didn't take long to register that I was tied
down; my movement was limited because I'd been restrained.
My ankles and wrists had padded straps wrapped around
them that were anchored to the bed frame, preventing my
mobility. I felt an instant surge of angry.

"Why am I tied up?" I hollered. I didn't know how close anyone was and I wasn't sure where the call button was located
so I figured I'd just yell. Someone ought to be listening, right?

I wasn't disappointed. Promptly, Carol came into the room
smiling, though less warmly than before. "You're awake."

"No shit, Sherlock! Why am I strapped to this bed?" I was
in no mood for trying to be sociable or nice.

"Here's the call button," Carol told me. "It's right beside
you, so you needn't holler."

"Why am I being restrained?" I asked again, ignoring any
show of hospitality the nurse tried to offer me.

I was tired of this bullshit. These people were supposed
to be here to help, but they didn't even listen. Even when I
told them the truth and the evidence obviously supported my
testimony, they chose to believe the lie. Apparently, no one
wanted to face reality. Was it easier to accept my mother's
story than to see her for what she really was?

My patience was gone. I was beyond caring what these people thought. They all believed I was crazy anyway. Funny,
that is exactly what I thought about them – hypocrites! It's so
easy to point the finger when it isn't directed at you.

"Calm down, Tiffany," Carol instructed gently, looking cautious. "You're only restrained for your own protection. We don't want anyone getting hurt here."

"I'm not going to hurt anyone," I snapped.

"Sweetie, you already have," she tried to remind me, giving a meaningful look towards my left arm.

"I didn't do that," I yelled yet again.

"Shhhh," she said trying to soothe me. "It's okay. You relax and I'll go get the doctor for you."

Carol made a hasty retreat from my room and I heard scuffling in the hallway. I knew that I needed to calm down or I'd never have a chance at making them hear me. Still, I was so worked up that I was finding it difficult to contain my anger. I was beyond tears and I just wanted to lash out; I didn't care at whom. No one cared about me so why should I care about them? Fair is fair, right?

I instantly felt horrible and sobered by a sense of shame in my own selfish thoughts. My anger dissipated to the point where I could at least manage it again. How many years had I been forced to control my feelings, to tuck them away as my mother commanded? I could do this. I could muster the strength to face this and to control myself so that I would at least get out of these damn straps.

As I lay there, waiting for someone to return to my room, I tried to see the situation from the perspective of the hospital staff. I thought about the wound my mother had caused to my forearm. Yeah, sadly I could see how someone might think it was self-inflicted. The angle of the knife coming down at me and the way I had positioned my arm to deflect the attack could make it seem like I did it myself.

Though I had my arm turned so that my palm faced my mother in a defensive move, the location of the wound made this questionable. The injury could have been inflicted in the same manner had my arm been facing towards me instead.

The fact that all vital ligaments and veins were missed would only add credence to the concept that the damage had been a calculated move I'd done to myself. Damn.

Alarm bells were sounding in my head now. If I didn't remain calm, my lack of emotional control would only add credibility to my mother's tale. I was sure I'd already caused enough damage to invalidate my story; I needed to try to repair the image people had of me. I was acting like a crazy person; at least from their point of view.

I realized that I had played the scene exactly the way my mom had intended me to. I'd been disconnected and lethargic initially, posing no resistance to her or her story. Then, as I recovered more and became more clear-headed, I had lost my temper and acted out in her favor. I had to give her props; my mother knew how to play the game. She could read people and situations, manipulating them for her benefit and I just made it that much easier for her.

I felt deflated and I closed my eyes as I took a deep breath. When I looked at it from an outside perspective, the presumed facts did not support me. I had a documented history of accidents and injuries, both in and away from my mother's presence. I had sustained enough damage from my arm wound to merit medical care, but not bad enough that I needed surgery. My mother was calm and calculating in her behavior and I was erratic in mine. What was I going to do now?

When the doctor entered the room, she was followed by my mother. All my efforts to control my anger were failing. I was instantly on full alert and my entire body tingled. My mother gave me a smug look that she quickly replaced with concern when the doctor turned to speak quietly to her. My mother stopped short then, holding her position. I knew the doctor had told her not to approach me too closely. How sweet.

It was truly touching how the doctor worried for my mother's well-being. I could see why she was in this field;

she was so thoughtful and sensitive. They made me want to vomit. This doctor was more of a half-wit than I thought. What the hell was she thinking bringing my mom in here?

Dr. Triton walked around the end of my bed, positioning herself between me and the window while my mother stood between me and the door. I never took my eyes off of my mother. My mother kept easy control of her appearance, though I could see her eyes were bright with amusement. That just made my anger rise to new heights.

"Get away from me," I snarled at my mom.

My mother gave a hurt expression and raised her hand to her mouth. I knew it was just an act, but the doctor fell for it, as expected. Looking horribly sad, my mother said, "Sweetie, I'm here because I love you. I only want to help you."

"Bullshit," I screamed as I pulled at the restraints. "You're so full of it."

"Tiffany, I just don't understand why you do these things," my mother said, feigning worry and dabbing at fake tears.

Dr. Triton called my attention by saying, "Tiffany, your mother and I thought it might help you to recall events better if you saw her in person."

I glared at Dr. Triton, showering her with all the pain, frustration, and heat that raged through my body. "Are you out of your fucking mind?"

I could see in Dr. Triton's face that she hadn't anticipated my reaction. Her mouth dropped open and her eyes were wide; she was clueless. It was a good thing they had strapped me down or else I probably would've punched the woman. I knew I would have at least attacked my mom. My step-dad wasn't there to intervene and Dr. Triton didn't appear capable of stopping me from making a move.

I screamed in frustration.

CHAPTER SEVEN

"You can't trust a god damn person – not even me," my mother was repeating her motto once again. She had a look of self-importance and I knew she was gloating.

My mother was a lot of things, but stupid was not one of them. She really knew how to read people, but I guess that is an important talent when you're a manipulator. Still, my mother was very strong and no matter what blows life threw at her, she always knew how to get back on her feet. I couldn't deny that I respected her strength and ingenuity.

"The only person you can count on in this world is your-self," she was saying.

I'd heard this speech before. I knew she had a valid point and though I could recite the oration by heart, I still listened to the lesson behind the words. Every fiber in my body told me the words were true. Didn't I have enough proof of that in my life? There was no knight in shining armor; no fairy god-mother to sprinkle magic on my life and make things better. There was me and only I could make my life what I wanted it to be.

Indubitably, I wouldn't have a say about my life until I was a legal adult. With my seventeenth birthday on the horizon, I felt excited that the time was short. However, being a realist, I understood that anything can happen in the space of a year. I also knew that if I didn't play my cards right, my mom would make sure something did happen. I could never let my guard down.

My mother drove us home as she lectured me about life through her eyes and values. I was happy enough that she was calm, but I knew the storm was brewing; it was simply a matter of time before it hit. When we got home, finally hidden behind the walls that ensured us privacy, I knew I'd face the anger my mother had been harboring. I'd embarrassed her and I'd allowed people to see behind her masquerade. She wouldn't just let that go. Undoubtedly, I would have a penalty to pay.

"It was so nice of that woman to stop and help you," my mother said with false pleasantry. I could tell the tide was turning and that she was having a harder time holding down her thirst for vengeance. "A lot of good it did you though, huh?"

When I had wandered aimlessly away from my mother's house after being raped, I'd felt numb. I had struggled to comprehend my mother's loyalty to Bill. It had baffled me that she allowed him to hurt me the way he did. I was just shocked that she'd allow someone else to damage something that was hers. I had assumed that she didn't know about Bill's intentions; maybe she had?

No, I didn't really believe that. No matter how cruel my mother could be, she'd never knowingly allow Bill to do such a thing, so why had she betrayed me by taking his side? I didn't even care that she was blaming me at that point; I was used to being blamed for the ills of the world. According to my mom, I was the reason there was rain instead of sunshine or night instead of day. I guess I was having trouble under-standing my mother's allegiance to Bill because his actions usurped her authority.

My mom was such a control freak that I figured Bill's at-tack on me would be seen as a personal attack on her. She coveted what other's had, but that didn't stop her from meticulously caring for her own possessions, one of which was me. I knew I was counted among my mom's possessions, as she reminded me many times; she'd always say that she "owned me" and therefore, she owned anything that was mine. Did that include my pain?

I wish I could have thought through things, but my mind was hazy. My brain was too foggy for me to really focus properly. Lost in my own confusion, I had stumbled along the roadside. I had no idea how much time had actually passed or exactly where I was; I just continued to move.

It felt good to be in motion and it seemed to help me shake off some of the anxiety that tormented my soul. Perhaps the fresh air would help to clear my head. When I stopped to look at something I had tripped on, a car driven by a worried-looking woman pulled up and parked beside me.

"Are you okay?" she asked anxiously.

I looked up blankly. Was I okay? I thought I was. I mean, it was only a chunk of earth that I had tripped on and I hadn't even fallen down. Usually, I'd take a big tumble because I was so clumsy, but I'd actually managed to remain on my feet this time. I was thrilled about that; it meant one less bruise to worry about later.

"Do you need to go to the hospital?" When she asked me this, I started paying a little more attention to her. After all, stumbling over an object didn't warrant a hospital visit. Perhaps I looked dreadful enough that it made her stop; more food for thought.

The woman looked to be in her late thirties or early forties. Her raven hair was pulled back in a long French braid that hung to about the middle of her back. She was clad in wine colored scrubs so she obviously knew where the hospital was. Yeah, that made perfect sense to me; I should go there. I kicked myself mentally for not thinking of it on my own. If nothing else, perhaps I'd be able to get cleaned up and rest until I decided where to go next.

"Honey, get in and I'll take you to the hospital," the lady told me.

As I approached the Honda Civic she was driving, I asked, "Are you on your way there now?"

"No, actually I just came from there," she replied. Seeing my concern she added, "It's okay though. It isn't far from here and I can help you."

"You don't mind?" I inquired. "I don't want to impose on you or your time."

She smiled warmly at me. "I don't mind at all and it's in no way an imposition. Come on; get in."

I'd gotten into the car with her. We arrived at the hospital and a whirlwind sucked me in. Everything happened around me as though I weren't really there; I didn't feel a part of it. I was asked a thousand questions, poked, prodded, and then some, but it seemed distant in a way. Thankfully, the lady stayed with me and often, she held my hand. I really liked her and appreciated her kindness. I was thankful for her presence - she felt like an anchor that kept me from flying away. I was so disconnected.

I was talking to a police officer when I saw my mother enter the emergency room and approach the nurses' station. I stopped speaking in mid-sentence and gapped at her in shock. The police officer looked at me and then followed my line of sight.

"Are you okay, miss? Do you know her?" he continued to question in his official way.

"That's my mother," I told him. I didn't say anything further and I never picked back up on the previous conversation we'd been engaged in.

"Hmm," I heard him say. "Well, well. I'd like to have a chat with her, if you don't mind."

I didn't care. I didn't think he really cared what my opinion was either, to be honest. He kept his eyes on my mother just as I did. I sensed the police officer shift in my peripheral vision and move away from me towards her. I didn't know what to expect, but I grasped the lady's hand tighter. I was thankful she was there with me though I didn't think she'd be able to do anything to help me. I didn't think anyone could and I ended up being right.

My mother had cried and carried on like any well-intended mother would after receiving the news that her daughter had been raped. She fought to be allowed to be with me and then doted on me when she finally convinced them to let her join me. I had completely shut down and my mother used that to her advantage, as was her nature. She told the medical staff and police that I had a documented history of mental instability and that being attacked probably thrust me into a delusional state.

I was in no shape to contradict my mother. I felt ancient and exhausted. I felt like a prisoner within myself and as if I was just watching a movie that was playing before my eyes. I just wanted all of it to end and disappear; I wanted to disappear.

I didn't like the attention I was getting and now that my mother had effectively convinced people of her version of events, she'd want to leave. That was an important element to her manipulations. Once she got her story to be accepted, she'd hide me away in order to avoid more questions and speculation. Even in my haze, I knew the longer I was held, the worse things would be when I finally got home.

I wasn't sure how to feel when the doctors said I'd be admitted into the hospital. I felt happy that I wouldn't be given over to my mother, but I was fearful of the potential reaction my mother would have. However, none of that mattered. My mom's own schemes back-fired and determined the outcome of this situation; neither of us would be able to change things.

Given my current mental state and considering my supposed mental history, the doctors said they needed to be sure I wasn't going to harm myself or anyone else. They decided to keep me under 48-hour lock up observation. After that time, I would be re-evaluated to assess whether or not I was stable enough to return home.

My mother fought eloquently to get them to reconsider, asking that I be placed into her care, but they said no. She quit trying to argue about it when she realized they weren't going to budge. So, I was processed into the mental ward and found myself in a barren little room with only minimal furnishings – all of which were made of hard plastic and rounded edges.

I had stuck to myself over the next days and didn't talk much. I did whatever was required of me so I could get out as soon as possible. I wasn't excited to get home, but I knew the longer I was there the worse my mom's wrath would be. I just wanted to get this over with and try to get back to normal, if that were even possible.

The lady who had brought me in had been a nurse named DiDi. She had stayed with me as long as she could, but when they processed me into the mental ward, I was no longer allowed to have visitors. When I entered through the secured entrance of the ward, I said farewell to DiDi for good. Though I didn't really know her, I knew I'd miss her terribly or at least the kindness she'd so generously shown me. I felt like my sole candle was blown out, leaving me in darkness.

When we arrived home, my mother barely threw the car into park before her mood completely soured. She said in a cold, bitter voice, "Hurry up and get your sorry ass into the house. I've had enough embarrassment to last a lifetime and I don't need you making more of a scene for the neighbors to gossip about."

Of course, our next door neighbors were out doing lawn work and stopped to watch our arrival. I kept my eyes to the ground and waited for my mother next to the front door. I just wanted to escape into our house, but I could hear my mother behind me as she cheerfully called greetings. I'd need to wait patiently for the performance to play out.

I heard the neighbor lady say, "Oh, good. You got her back home."

My mother was telling her how relieved she was to have me home. Apparently, my mother had suffered greatly through this trying time, getting so upset she couldn't eat or sleep. The neighbors were hanging on her every word and consoling her with every lead she gave them. It was a well-choreographed dance that made me want to vomit.

When my mother felt like she'd gotten enough pampering from her sympathetic "friends", she made her excuses, saying she wasn't supposed to leave me unsupervised. When we entered the house and my mom shut the door behind us, I began trembling with anxiety over what was to come. I sighed deeply, knowing it'd be a long night ahead.

I was already exhausted, but I had a sneaky suspicion my weariness was more of an emotional state than a physical one. I walked through the house and simply sat down at the table, waiting for mother. My stomach knotted up as she put her purse and keys away. The knotting caused physical pain as my mother turned her full attention to me.

***

Did everyone really believe I had done this to myself? They must have if they'd allowed my mother into the room with me; she wasn't supposed to be able to go further onto the ward than the day room. If they had thought she had actually harmed me, they'd have kept her from me; arrested her. I honestly had a moment of uncertainty. Maybe I did trust them more than I should.

What had the medical staff or police officers done to earn my trust? What had *anyone* done to earn my trust? Nothing; they'd done nothing to earn my trust or my respect. They didn't listen to me and they sure as hell didn't protect me. Why did I even try then? Of course, in asking the question, I'd already known the answer; faith. I hoped; I couldn't help it.

I had faith that a better day would be born. I had hope that someone would see my plight and maybe not rescue me, but show me how to get myself out of trouble. I had to believe that people were innately good or at least better than my mother and step-dad. I had to believe that there were more people like DiDi in the world or I might as well give up all together.

I freaked out, energized by a renewed vigor when my mother tried to get near to me. I cursed her and the stupid doctor. I wanted nothing more than to lash out at them both, but the restraints held me back. That only frustrated me more and I growled in rage, yanking at the bonds holding my arms and legs with all the strength I could muster.

I must have been throwing quite the fit as the nursing staff came running. Rhonda looked angry as she entered the room and took inventory of who was present. She called out to a Dr. Maxwell and quickly ushered my mother from the room along with an uncertain looking Dr. Triton. Good riddance; I was glad to see them go!

The big burly black man, Timothy – the same one who had helped sedate me earlier – assisted Rhonda in dragging my belligerent mother and dumb-founded doctor out. Carol and Charlotte came in to try to calm me. They were followed closely by a stately-looking tall, middle-aged man; Dr. Maxwell, I presumed.

I was still worked up, but I was more reserved once my mother and Dr. Triton had left. Dr. Maxwell was watching the situation like a hawk and I knew he didn't miss a thing. I felt nervous under his watchful eye, but not threatened. When

Charlotte asked him if he wanted to give me a sedative, he said no.

"You're not going to be giving us any more trouble, are you Tiffany?" he asked me, looking directly at me in a kindly manner.

I shook my head no. I focused on my breathing and tried to temper my shaking. Involuntary tears dripped down my face and I lay back, wishing to be invisible. It was embarrasing to be crying in front of these people. I felt weak and humiliated.

"Charlotte," Dr. Maxwell said, "Please tell Dr. Triton to meet me in my office in 10 minutes and make sure Tiffany's mother is removed from the ward."

"Yes, Doctor," she replied and quickly left the room.

Carol was rubbing my arm in an attempt to soothe me. She was cooing lightly, but her body was stiff with tension. I saw the look she and Dr. Maxwell exchanged and I knew that there was going to be hell to pay, but I wasn't sure who would receive the bill. I hoped I wasn't the recipient of it. After all, I knew their expressions well; disappointment and displeasure.

"Are you okay now?" Carol asked me sweetly. Her tension eased in direct relation to my own. I nodded at her as I exhaled loudly. Carol dabbed a tissue at my face to try to mop up some of the tears.

Dr. Maxwell began to remove my restraints. As he did, he eyed me severely and said, "I'm going to trust you to behave, Tiffany. I'll be sure to keep your mother away -"

"And Dr. Triton," I said in a weak, shaky voice. I felt bad cutting him off, but I wanted to be certain of my wishes. I wanted no doubt.

Dr. Maxwell nodded while Carol began helping to undo my ties, "And Dr. Triton, but I can't have any more of these outbursts. Do you understand?"

Again, I nodded. I looked sadly at Carol who in turn smiled at me reassuringly and patted my hand gently. "What's going to happen now?" I wondered out loud.

"Well," Dr. Maxwell said frankly, "I'm going to replace Dr. Triton as your primary psychiatrist and we're going to see if we can make you feel better."

"Are you going to arrest my mother?"

"No," he told me. "We don't have enough evidence to support your story." I looked at him in alarm. He read my face clearly and included, "or hers."

I started to cry harder. At least now I was untied and could blow my snotty nose and wipe my own tears. I sat up, pulled my knees into my chest, and wrapped my arms around my legs. I buried my face in my knees.

"This is never going to end, is it?" I asked in hopelessness.

"We're going to do everything we can to help you," Dr. Maxwell assured me. "I promise."

I looked up into the doctor's eyes and demanded to know, "but there's not a lot you can do, is there?"

Dr. Maxwell was unable to respond, but I already knew the answer. My breath caught in my throat and I choked on my own tears. Carol made gentle *shushing* sounds at me and Dr. Maxwell squeezed my hand. Then he patted my shoulder closest to him and told me that he was going to leave me in Carol's capable hands. With that, he exited the room.

I could hear a bit of an uproar in the hallway. I could hear my mother's voice as she complained and threatened to sue; demanding to see me. Dr. Maxwell was telling her that Dr. Triton had breached protocol when she allowed my mother into my room. Visitors were strictly regulated and only allowed in the day room or around the nurse's station. He continued by saying the protocols were in place for everyone's safety.

I heard my mother continue to protest, but Dr. Maxwell told her in no uncertain terms that she'd no longer be allowed on the ward at all. He said that the first priority was my health and until I could work through the ordeal, he felt it was best to keep me in isolation. I knew my mother wouldn't take this well, but I was greatly relieved.

After that, I heard a bit more stomping and ruckus as the hushed voices moved further away from my room. Eventually, the sound of a heavy door slamming shut. The boom rang through the halls, reaching my ears and I knew my mother was finally gone. If nothing more was done, I was grateful for the serenity of that moment.

I cried myself out and eventually fell asleep from the exhaustion that consumed me. I think someone tried to wake me at one point for a dinner, but I couldn't pull myself into consciousness enough to respond. I lay locked in fitful dreams of my tyrannical mother in a wicked witch's costume, like you'd see in a rendition of "Snow White." In my dream, my mother was battling a warrior clad Dr. Maxwell.

When I woke later that night, the hospital unit was quiet. I rolled towards the window and gazed at the few lights I could see as they decorated the metropolis. I understood that Dr. Maxwell wasn't my prince charming or any sort of knight in shining armor. Still, it felt good to believe that someone was finally fighting on my behalf.

As I lay in the late hours of night or perhaps the wee hours of morning, I felt content. I'd been right to keep faith and trust when I had no reason to. I didn't expect any grand gestures or magical solutions to things, but my hope was fueled. Perhaps this was where I'd be taking that first step towards freedom from my oppressors.

CHAPTER EIGHT

"That's not clean enough," my mother stormed. She stomped over to the bookcase and started to pull novels off the shelf. "You have to move everything; clean underneath and behind the books then dusty them off before putting them away."

My mother was in full OCD mode. She had times when she'd get a bug up her ass and she'd go on a psycho cleaning frenzy, but this time was different. This time, I was the source of the contamination and she just couldn't make me clean enough. Since Bill had soiled me in ways she couldn't clean, she felt like I was now infecting her home with unseen germs.

My mother forced me to shower at least three times a day. My skin was getting so dry and rough despite the lotion I was using. The only reason my hair was holding up was because I had a good conditioner. I could only imagine how much worse the effects would have been if we hadn't had a water softener.

In between my mandated personal hygiene regiment, I was forced to scrub the house. As with everything, my mother had a specific way that it had to be done. If it wasn't performed exactly her way or to her standards, I'd have to start again. I wouldn't redo the one task that was unsatisfactory, but rather, an error meant I had to go back to the start. The first step was always to shower so I'd be clean; thereby, avoiding additional contamination.

My mother made me pre-clean for cleaning, just as I had to do when doing dishes. After I showered then I cleaned the room where I'd be moving all the furnishings from the dirty room. This was done to make sure I didn't make the dirty items dirtier. In an effort to avoid dragging dirt back and forth from room to room, a towel was folded neatly between the thresholds that connected the rooms. I was to wipe my feet off as I passed through the doorway, whether entering or exiting.

Once the proposed room for cleaning was emptied, I was to scrub and disinfect everything. I washed windows and bleached baseboards. I swept, vacuumed, and mopped the floor. I always worked my way top down in an effort to preserve the cleanliness of areas that I had already addressed. This held true when showering as well; you always shampooed and then washed from your face down to your feet. If you washed in reverse then all your efforts would be null and void; you'd have to start again.

Once I cleaned the room to my mother's satisfaction, the next step was to wash and disinfect the furnishings I'd be returning to the newly-cleaned room. You cannot bring dirty items into a clean room or you'd defeat your purpose. Dirty items would just leave dirt and dust in their wake, rendering the room to be filthy. So, I worked to wipe, wash, and polish as directed, all the while wiping my feet in between rooms as I moved back and forth.

Once I had the desired room cleaned to perfection, it was time to re-clean the room I had scrubbed as a staging area for the furnishings. Though this room had already been tended to, it was now dirty since I had brought all the dusty items here to wash. So, my next step was to clean this room to the same standards as the previous room.

My final step was always to re-shower. Although I had showered before my chores, the act of cleaning had caused me to be contaminated. I was not only covered in cleaning chemicals, but I had become dirty from my contact with the dusty items. Therefore, before I was allowed to enter any other room, I had to strip, putting my clothes directly into the washing machine and shower all over again.

When everything was finally done, I was free to hide in my room. It was quite an ordeal and I never got to my room quickly enough. Even when I finally did reach my room, it didn't guarantee anything. Depending on my mother's mood, I could be called to attend another chore. However, being out-of-sight usually helped to keep me out-of-mind.

In this moment, I was only at the "washing the furnishings" stage. Unfortunately, I still had a long night ahead of me. It didn't matter that I'd have to get up for class in the morning; I wouldn't be allowed to sleep until everything was just right. Honestly, it wouldn't be the first time I went without sleep if I didn't finish in time to make it to bed.

My mother had a propensity for staying up late. This was her favorite time to be inspired to do things. It wasn't unusual for her to rouse me from my bed in the middle of the night to do some task that apparently just couldn't wait until morning. Often, it was laundry, but sometimes it was deep cleaning or even painting; whatever triggered her fancy in that moment.

"Vacuum off that lamp shade," she ordered, "and don't forget to wipe off the lamp itself."

I knew what she expected, just as she was fully aware that I knew. Still, she had to dominate; she had to control. She'd hover over me, micromanaging; supervising everything I did down to the minutest element, but she wouldn't do the task herself. That was unless she decided to make a lesson of it. That was when she'd ridicule me for my ineptitude and take me step-by-step through the proper procedures; no one wanted that.

Despite her having done the task, she would make me repeat the chore after her. She'd watch to see that I followed her instructions precisely, making sure I understood for "next time". Often I was forced to repeat the process several times before she accepted that I had understood. By the end of it all, she'd have released all of her tension and the anxiety that had fueled her would have been spent. Maybe she was manic depressive?

I never knew when these nights would occur and I never knew if she'd come back to make me do something more. I would always end up exhausted, but too keyed up to sleep, so it didn't really matter whether I got to bed or not. On the nights I actually made it to bed, I'd lie awake for a while, just listening. When I'd finally find my slumber, it was just in time for my alarm to go off for school.

"Pick that up better than that," mother demanded. "You're going to drag shit round and then we'll have to start all over again."

We; We, my ass! She meant me and to my dismay, she was serious. I worked diligently to try to hurry this night along, but I took painstaking efforts to ensure everything was perfect. I certainly didn't want to start the process all over again; I wanted to go to bed. I was already asleep on my feet as it was. My mother might get to sleep all day, but I most certainly didn't.

I rechanneled my energies. Instead of being angry and resentful, I pushed the emotions into driving my efforts. I hated having my mother following me around, breathing so close to my face. I swear she had no sense of personal space, at least not where I was concerned. The only way to end this bullshit was to finish it, so I worked like a mule.

It was about 3:00 AM when I – excuse me, *we* – finished. I was sore and my hands hurt from all the chemicals. I was just about to hit the showers when my step-dad meandered into the room. He'd been out with some friends which was probably the reason for my mother's enterprising OCD. He'd obviously been drinking. His smell wafted across the room, overpowering the cleaner materials.

He staggered over to my mother with the obvious intent of kissing her. When he got near her, she pushed him away from her, repulsed. Though he caught his balance before he tumbled to the ground, he tripped over the dirty mop bucket, spilling its contents across the clean floors. My eyes opened wide and I gasped loudly.

"Fuckin' A!" my mother exclaimed in annoyance. "What the hell is wrong with you? Go to bed, you jackass." My step-dad chortled and my mother waved him off after allowing him to kiss her cheek softly.

"Sorry; sorry," he chirped happily and unsteadily. My mother just indulged him as he slowly trotted away.

When he exited the room and entered into the kitchen, my mother looked at me sternly. She eyed me like I'd staged the whole calamity just to be insubordinate. I sighed deeply as my mother said the words I already knew to expect "start over."

***

"Stupid, stupid, girl," my mother taunted me. "When will you ever learn?"

I knew better than to speak. This was an attempt to provoke me into some display of emotion that my mother could use against me. That was also why I never wrote anything down. My mother would rummage through my stuff, hoping to find some sort of damning evidence of disobedience. I'd go to extremes to deny her that privilege.

I had taken it to heart when she'd told me that if it was something she couldn't see then it never should have been written in the first place. Whether it had been written by my hand or another's made no difference; the result was the same, if found. If something existed that opposed her, I was there to pay the price. There was always a price, even for the good things in life.

"You know none of them believe you anyway," she cackled. "You're just wasting everyone's time."

I maintained my meek composure; docile in every way. My mother was like a wild creature, demanding that I avoid direct eye contact. To look at her would be to challenge her and I never wanted to do that, especially in a confined space such as the car. Besides, it wasn't like I had any power; I was nothing. Even if I hadn't known I was powerless from the way my pleas for help were ignored, my mother's heavy hand had reminded me enough times to keep me silent.

"You'll never prove I did anything," she said in a cocky tone. "You'll only make them think you're crazy, like I've said."

She was probably correct in her assessment of the situation, but what could I do? Nothing; I could do nothing because I was nothing. At least that was what she wanted me to believe and stupid me, I bought into what she was selling. More often than not, I felt like nothing. My own acceptance of it is what truly made me nothing and though I knew that, I couldn't seem to change it.

"This is a waste of time," my mother complained as we pulled into the parking lot of Dr. Maxwell's office. "This man can't do anything for you. Nobody can or they already would have."

She had a point there, for sure. No one seemed to be able to do anything contrary to my mother's wishes. Whether they believed me or not didn't change the outcome either. Dr. Maxwell was living proof of that. He was the one person in the world who seemed to agree with me about my mother, but that didn't give him anything, but frustration.

As my mother threw the car into park, she turned to look at me. She waited until I grudgingly made eye contact with her then she said firmly, "I own you."

I wondered whether she were right. Do all parents actually own their children, but we just don't acknowledge it out loud because of social protocols? I did feel more like a possession of hers than a child; I was something to tame and control. I didn't feel loved, just conquered.

My parents were always there to escort me to my appointments. Hell, they escorted me everywhere; treating me like a prisoner. Of course, they were never allowed into the room when I had my therapy sessions, but that didn't stop my mother from making her presence known. She was quite the attention whore.

The way she would huff and puff, constantly checking the time. The rude comments she'd make to the receptionist and the complaints she'd vocalize to my step-dad were simply embarrassing. I wanted to hide behind something, especially when she turned her disappointment towards me. After all, it was my fault she had to waste her precious time at this god-forsaken place.

Sitting on the cushioned chair in Dr. Maxwell's office, I questioned my perception of reality. I wondered whether I really was the horrible person my mother portrayed me as. Perhaps I truly was the burden she claimed and I just didn't want to see it. I mean, no one wants to acknowledge themselves as an inferior, tawdry, or worthless person, right?

Perhaps I really was disillusioned; unable to see myself for who, and what, I really was. Maybe I really was an ungrateful wretch who just refused to take responsibility for my own actions. Maybe I was lying to myself because I didn't want to admit to being a bad person. Maybe. . .

"What are you thinking about?" Dr. Maxwell asked as he took in my pensive expression.

"I'm wondering if she's right," I said quietly.

"About what, exactly?" my doctor pulled at the threads for more detail.

"Maybe I *am* the problem," I told him. "Maybe I can't tell what's real. I mean, truth is subjective, right? How do I know that my version of the truth is the correct one?"

"You know the truth," he told me. "You have the scars to prove it."

"Do I?" I questioned. "If I do, they aren't setting me free."

"They will," Dr. Maxwell tried to reassure me.

"Maybe," I said doubtfully, "or maybe she's right."

"She's not right," he told me. Though he sounded confident when he said it, I think we both had our doubts.

"And yet, here I sit," I pointed out. "I'm treated like a prisoner in my own home. Hell, I'm treated worse than a prisoner; at least they have rights."

"You don't really believe that," Dr. Maxwell gently chided.

I looked down at my hands and admitted, "You know, there are times when I'm unsure about what's happening around me. There are times when I feel like it's all a dream and I can't really discern if I'm even awake, let alone what's real."

Dr. Maxwell looked at me with understanding, "That's how it is when you have anxiety attacks. We've talked about this before."

He was right. We had discussed all of it before, but my doubt was still there. My mother made sure the doubt was there. All she needed was a small foot-hold, a crack in my certainty. As brittle as I always felt, she never failed to find the kink in my armor.

"My mother says that I'm telling the truth," I told him. "She says that I'm not really lying since I believe in what I'm saying. She tells people that I blame her because in my mind, I really believe it; it's my reality and therefore, not a real lie."

Dr. Maxwell gave me a moment to swim in my self-pity then he said, "Are you done?"

I looked at him guiltily, "Yeah; sorry. It's just it would be so much easier if I just accepted things the way she wants me to."

"That's probably right; it would be easier," he reaffirmed, "but it still doesn't make it reality. We both know that she's the one lying."

"Yet she has everyone's support," I pouted in sadness.

"Not everyone's," Dr. Maxwell pointed out with a gentle smile.

I tried to smile back, but my heart wasn't in it. I appreciated Dr. Maxwell, but that doubt was still there picking at my almost non-existent confidence. "I'm afraid of doing something," I confessed.

"What do you mean," the doctor asked me.

"When I'm in the haze caused by my anxiety," I explained, "I'm afraid I'll confuse things and do something, thinking it's a dream when it's not."

"Like what?"

"I don't know. Sometimes I have these impulses," I explained. "Sometimes I have the urge to do such horrible things."

"We all have those. It's normal," the doctor stated.

"That may be true, but acting on them isn't and that's what I'm talking about," I countered. "Sometimes I just want to reach out and hurt her back. Sometimes I almost do."

"That's understandable," he said, "you're angry. It's a normal instinct to want to lash out at whatever corners you."

"I don't want to be like her," I said barely more than a whisper. "If I can't control my feelings or if I do something when I think I'm dreaming though I'm not. . . "

I shook my head sadly, ending my verbal contemplation. I knew that Dr. Maxwell didn't have all the answers or a magic cure to end all that ailed me. Still, it was nice to be able to talk. It was a surprisingly simple way to let go of some of the steam that built up inside me. It was a safe way to counter my darker desires and to confront my personal demons.

Dr. Maxwell was encouraging and accepting; he never judged me. I got that it was his job to be neutral and to help me explore the circus inside my head, but it still felt good. It felt good to have someone say such positive things to me. It felt good to have someone care about what I thought and felt; to really listen to my words. Even if that was a falsehood, I didn't care as long as the doctor kept up the appearance of active participation in our conversations together. That was enough for me.

"You know, I don't want to be a victim," I told him.

"I know and I don't think you are," he told me. "You don't ask for sympathy and you don't give up."

I looked at him and responded, "Sometimes I want to. Sometime I want to lie down and never get back up. Sometimes I want to die."

"But you don't," Dr. Maxwell points out. "You keep going. No matter what life, nay, your mother throws at you, you keep going."

I looked at him, temporarily thrown off from our conversational course. "Did you really just say 'nay" in a sentence?" I laughed, but no joy was in the sound.

Looking slightly embarrassed, Dr. Maxwell replied, "Yes, I guess I did." He smiled to himself, glad to have a moment's reprieve from the tension.

After a brief pause, I said, "She says I'm stupid. I think she's right."

"She's not and you're not stupid. Tiffany, you're a survivor," he championed me.

"I'm not sure I want to be," I remarked. "If surviving is all there is to living, I don't think I want to continue to be a part of it."

As he looked at me, I could tell that there were many things Dr. Maxwell wanted to say to me. He probably wanted to blow sunshine up my ass, but to his credit, he didn't. He didn't try to correct me or tell me what I should do or feel. Instead, he finally said, "It is okay to feel the way you do. You have a right to feel everything and anything you want."

"I know," I retorted. "I've known that was the one thing no one could take from me. Still, I don't like to feel this way, but I can't seem to change things. I mean, until I can change the situation of my existence, I can't change the content of my emotional repertoire."

Dr. Maxwell simply nodded in acknowledgement of my statement. To the core of my being, I felt that he believed me; believed my side of the stories told. I knew he just wanted to help, but his abilities to help were greatly limited. There were technicalities and rules that had to be followed. There were laws that dictated invisible boundaries and evidence that had to stand up to strict guidelines.

Where I was in my life was where I'd be for a long time yet; maybe forever. Though I was just about to turn seventeen years old, the countdown was on to my eighteenth birthday. I didn't expect anything earth-shattering to happen when I finally did reached that landmark, but I knew it'd mean I could leave quietly in the night. It would mean no one could force me back to my prison or make me stay with my mom any longer. It couldn't come quickly enough.

Thinking about that day and anticipating the independence it promised was almost physically painful. My chest constricted and it seemed like it was so far off in the future; almost unattainable. Also, I knew that it wouldn't be an easy day either. I was certain it would be a day of great battle; probably the worst one I ever have to fight.

Sitting there, I wasn't convinced I'd survive until that day let alone beyond it. I felt the struggle intensifying between my mom and me no matter what I did to try to stop it. I couldn't imagine a future where she'd just let me walk away from her. As it was, I felt like she was breaking me down a little more each day.

"I don't know how much more I can take," I confessed. "I feel like I'm disappearing. Every day she kills me a little more."

"Yet you're here," he reassured me.

"Today, but what about tomorrow?" I asked him. "She's erasing me bit by bit and it's painfully obvious that no one can stop her."

"You can. You *will*," Dr. Maxwell seemed so sure. Maybe he was the one who was disillusioned.

CHAPTER NINE

The bruises and pain from my mother's beating simply blended into the rest of the damage visible on my body. No one would be the wiser and my mother was a lot happier having released her tensions punishing me. I felt better that the situation was finally at a close. We'd be able to move forward to some extent now though I knew things would never truly be over; not for me anyway. I'd bear the scars of this event for the rest of my life; even when they faded from sight, they'd remain etched into my memory.

In some ways, it wasn't so bad. I say that because in many ways we ignored what had happened. Not a lot changed in my world; even the increased duties and chores weren't out of the ordinary really. My mother enjoyed being able to make me do things I didn't like or want to do as a form of punishment. The constant work made it easy for me to focus on something other than past events.

The hardest times were when I was alone. I imagined sounds and jumped at shadows created by the car lights moving outside the windows. I felt depressed and there was a pressure on my chest that felt like someone was sitting on me; like he was sitting on me. It made it hard to breathe, which was physically painful. I'd work to focus on my breathing, but it was hard to regulate my breath when the tears began.

Not a night passed that I didn't cry. My body was healing from the trauma in good measure, but my mind was a mess. I was restless and frightened, unable to sleep or at least sleep without dreams of Bill haunting me. I often woke in a cold sweat, shaking from anxiety. I kept telling myself it would get better with time. I just hoped it didn't take too long.

Over the next few weeks, I started feeling weaker; I was exhausted in ways I'd never known before. I didn't pay it much attention, thinking it was just a natural result of the extra chores my mother tasked me as my penance. When I was able to sleep, I was restless and plagued with nightmares. Mostly, I suffered from insomnia so naturally, I assumed this was the reason I had become so run down. I never considered any other explanation.

When I began getting sick, I just assumed I was catching some sort of bug. After all, my immune system was compromised from my insomnia and it was flu season. It wasn't until I missed my period that I worried. I was terrified as the reality of what was happening to me penetrated my understanding. I started to shake uncontrollably and began vomiting all the more intensely.

I wanted to purge myself of this reality. I wanted to wake up and find this was all just another nightmare. Oh, God, how could this be happening? What would this mean? My biggest concern was my mother's reaction.

My fear of my mother over-shadowed my personal feelings about the situation. My feelings really didn't matter anyway. I had no doubt that all decisions would be made by my mother. I was hers to command, right?

I couldn't believe that I was pregnant. I was barely seventeen years old and the only time I'd ever had sex was when my step-dad's best friend raped me. I puked again and my head started pounding with pain. How was I going to tell my mother?

I felt so conflicted. As I thought through various scenarios, I came to realize that my mother wasn't my biggest concern. I had an epiphany about myself and it changed everything for me. In that one moment, I realized that the only thing that mattered was my baby.

I feared my mom my whole life and I had worried that I'd grow into a replica of her. I decided that this baby would give me strength to break free from all of that apprehension. I didn't really know what that meant or how it would come to be, but I knew that I would be different. Life was no longer about me, but rather, it was about protecting my baby from my mother.

I was agitated all day and quite jumpy. I was trying to decide what to do and how to do it. I knew I needed to eventually tell my mother, but I was terrified by the ramifications of this news and the potential repercussions it would yield. Still, I had to be sure to do what was right for my baby and that meant I needed to seek healthcare. In order to do that, I needed to involve my mom.

True to her controlling nature, my mother kept all of my personal documents locked away. I didn't have access to my insurance information or my physician's contact data. The only clinics I knew I could go to without my mother's involvement were abortion clinics and that was never a viable option.

I believed all life was divinely inspired and planned. I may not have liked how I got pregnant, but it wasn't my fault and it most certainly wasn't the baby's fault. I would *not* punish my child for things that were out of its control. I would *not* be my mother and I would *not* want to make my child feel the way my mother made me feel - ever.

I would see this pregnancy through and then give my baby up for adoption. I'd give it a chance to have a better life than I could provide; a life away from my mother. No path had ever been made clearer to me than the one that was now stretched out before me. The only way to protect my baby was to give my baby away.

Some lessons are learned through positive reinforcement. Other lessons are learned by realizing what *not* to do in order to be a better person. Most of my lessons were learned in this backwards manner; through exposure to undesirable behaviors. I saw in my mother the things I never wanted to perpetuate within myself and that made it easy for me to discern my course of action. I'd do whatever I had to in order to see my decision come to fruition.

Having to watch people's body language and read between their words for their real meaning made me more sensitive to behaviors. I paid closer attention to nuances overlooked by others. I was more conscious of what to do and what not to do; of who I was, who I had the potential to be, and who I wanted to become. It was a sad reality, but it was my reality. I didn't have to like it, but I'd learn and grow not only from it, but beyond it.

Acknowledging that I was pregnant somehow gave me a strength I never knew I had inside me. I felt like I had a purpose and it strengthened my conviction to be more than I was. I had a reason to fight and to build the life my child deserved to live. Those feelings made me determined and strong enough to face my mother.

My mother took the news better than I had expected which put me immediately on alert. My mother was too calculating a person to seem so nonchalant about my condition. I had expected World War III to happen and instead, I got *affection*. My mother actually kissed me in congratulation and hugged me in joy. She was actually pleased that I was going to have a child. I never saw that coming.

My mother continued to treat me with love and tenderness over the next few days. She actually pampered me and joked with me; she took an avid interest in my life and smiled at me often. I was completely floored and I had no idea what to make of her change of heart. Although I wanted to enjoy her generosity and warmth, I remained deeply suspicious. It was such a conflict of emotions and it caused me incredible stress.

Light dawned as to what was causing my mother's joy when Bill showed up at our door one day. He wouldn't look at me at all which suited me just fine. When he did look in my direction, he looked around or through me. As far as he was concerned, I was invisible. I really didn't mind though. I welcomed his distance, feeling sick to even have him in the same house with me. I escaped as soon as my mother allowed me to take my leave.

My mom and step-dad were engaged in some intense conversation with Bill. I eavesdropped as best I could while remaining in my room and it didn't take me long to understand what the exchange was about. They were planning financial arrangements for my care; for the baby. They were negotiating monies that would, of course, be given to my parents and not to me or to the baby. Bill looked ill and my mother, triumphant. I understood my worth to my mother now; I was her access to Bill's wealth.

My mother's plan was to blackmail Bill. She hadn't wanted to side with me on the rape because she wanted to stay in Bill's good graces. She was happy being saddled up to his money and wanted his tribute to her to continue. His clout in the business world somehow gave her a sense of place and status while his gifts placated her. When she realized that I was pregnant, she found a new way to up her own clout and to dip deeper into Bill's assets.

She was calculating a future where she'd live in comfort at Bill's expense. Of course, none of it had anything to do with me or my baby beyond the surface; we were simply the means to her ends. We represented the living proof of his indiscretion; the indiscretion that would be the leverage my mother needed to get everything she wanted from Bill.

I knew unequivocally that Bill would agree to anything my mother suggested. If he didn't then she would surely press rape charges; my trip to the ER was clear evidence of that attack though my mom made certain I never told who'd done it. Now, Bill would have to do more to appease my mom in order to protect himself. He'd do it happily in order to prevent his name and status from being tarnished.

I sat in my bedroom quietly. I absently stroked my little bump and felt sad. I already loved this being inside me and that made me all the more certain of its future. It'd need to get away from here, away from her, as soon as possible. I knew that this would cause problems with my mother's plans for Bill and his hefty bank account, but I wasn't going to let her use my child the way she used me.

It hurt me terribly to think of what I needed to do, but I wouldn't be able to live with myself if I didn't let my baby go. My feelings were inconsequential; my baby deserved a real life. If I were to be any sort of mother, it'd be the kind of mom who put the needs of my child before her own. I knew without question that what my baby needed most was to be removed from us all.

***

"Happy birthday," Dr. Maxwell said happily, smiling warmly at me.

I returned his smile and said, "Thanks."

"So, it seems like things are going better for you lately," he noted.

"Yeah," I sighed. "I can't complain."

"But. . ." the doctor coaxed me for more.

"But what?" I asked.

The doctor gave me a knowing look. "You say you can't complain, *but...*" He gestured to me to fill in the rest of the sentence.

"But nothing," I replied.

"But *something*," he countered.

I looked away in annoyance. I knew I could complain, but I didn't want to. I was grateful that I wasn't being beaten up and thankful that my mom had actually thrown me a birthday party; the first party since my grandma passed away. Still, things just felt wrong; I felt uneasy.

"I can do this all day, you know," Dr. Maxwell challenged. I sighed and rolled my eyes.

"I don't want to complain, *but...*" I said, exaggerating the last word. "I guess I'm just not used to being treated properly. Things are just so different and I feel so out of my element that it's unnerving."

"You're worried she's up to something," he guessed.

"She's always up to something," I reminded him. "It's just, this time her plot includes my baby and not just me."

"You think your mother's going to hurt the baby?"

"No, actually I don't," I said, surprising him. "I think the baby is worth too much to her for that."

"You think she's going to revert back to hurting you," he understood.

"Yes, once the baby is born," I confirmed his suspicions.

"Why?"

"It's the only thing that makes sense to me. The only worth I have to her is this baby. Unfortunately, this baby is worth everything to her, so I know she's going to try to take it from me," I said sadly. "She's going to try to control it even more than she ever controlled me."

"What if you're wrong? What if things genuinely are improving?" he questioned.

"I would love to be wrong, but I'm not. Everything has a price tag when it comes to my mom and I think my baby is going to be the price she demands for her kindness."

"Are you sure?" he asked though I could see he already knew the truth of my words.

"Positive," I told him. "The thing is that I just haven't figured out what to do about it yet."

"You have every possibility available to you," he encouraged me.

"I wish that were true," I said with a heavy heart, "but we both know better than that. My mom is never going to let this baby go. She may let me go because of the baby, but this baby is her treasure trove."

Dr. Maxwell looked sad and as if he'd aged greatly in the short time I'd known him. I knew my case weighed heavily on his mind and that he suffered from bouts of guilt. He was almost as discouraged as me. Almost.

"When the time comes, I know I'm going to need your help," I informed him.

"I'll do whatever I can. I'm just sorry that I don't have more authority to save you from this all right now," he confessed.

"It's okay," I told him. "It's not your fault, but if you really want to do something to make it up to me, then give me your unconditional promise that you'll do whatever I decide is right for my baby. I don't want any shit about it; no lectures. Promise me you'll support and implement whatever I choose to do."

Dr. Maxwell nodded his sad agreement. With that settled, I needed to decide what my plan would be. I knew it would involve giving my baby up for adoption, but I needed to research things more. I needed more information before I'd share any details about my intentions or thoughts.

CHAPTER TEN

I was at the end of my first trimester. I wasn't really showing yet save for a tiny bump where my skinny belly was starting to fill out some. My mother was convinced it meant I was having a baby boy. This thrilled her, as she said a daughter was "all drama."

My mom was starting to look into baby names she liked. She told me that I could pick from the list of her favorites. She was feeling generous in allowing me to have a say in my baby's name since I was the birth mom, after all. Of course, she already had ideas of how the baby would be a "grandma's boy" and how they'd conspire against me. I just kept silent.

It was nice to see my mom happy, but I knew she was excited for all the wrong reasons. Instead of being pleased that she'd be a grandma, she was looking forward to teaching my baby to ridicule me. She was pleased with the idea that her and my child would be a team; a team against me. Apparently, the lesson of "honoring thy mother and thy father" would simply be altered to, "It's all about grandma."

I was relieved that my mom was so positive about the baby and that she wanted to be so involved, but her reasoning just reinforced my convictions. Instead of wishing the best for my baby, she was planning how she was going to spend the increased income Bill would be contributing because of his indiscretion. She spoke of the baby like it was a toy she'd

113

play with and then give back to me when it was no longer fun for her. I was always pictured as the dim-witted servant girl who'd play nanny and maid.

My mom seemed so unrealistic when it came to her hopes for the future. I guess I should have felt grateful that she included me in her visions at all, but I was sure that would combust into ash once she discovered I had given the baby up for adoption. I was still uncertain about how I would make it happen and I was worried about my mom intervening in the whole process.

I felt nauseated most days. Though I knew I was sick from worry and disgust with my mother, I passed it off as morning sickness. This seemed the safest excuse for my frequent bathroom trips. I fretted more than not, agonizing over what I could do to protect my baby. I didn't think it'd be enough to just give up parental rights. What if my mom made a plea to be the adoptive parent based on her blood relation?

When I was at school, I would take lunch in the library. This gave me uninhibited and unmonitored time to research things I wanted to know. I had started to formulate a plan, but I knew I was going to need help to make it a reality. I just didn't know the best way to go about everything, and my time and resources were limited.

My mother would use everything in her arsenal against me once she realized I intended to take the baby from her. She would use my history of supposed mental instability and my lack of financial independence to take custody of my baby. She would have all the resources at her disposal to get the results she wanted, and then get my baby to hold over me.

Bill could be an issue since he was the biological father. Still, I doubted that he'd push anything since my mom threatened to press rape charges. If Bill openly admitted to being the baby's father, my mom would ruin him in every way possible; not just by social reputation, but financially as well. I had no doubt in my mind that he'd simply try to disappear into the shadows of obscurity. Though he could be an issue, I knew he wouldn't be.

As it was, my mom was still negotiating whether or not to put him on the birth certificate. It was a ploy for her to bleed more out of Bill than he wanted to give. In the end, I knew his name would be omitted from the legalities and the baby's father would be listed and "unknown." This would ensure my mother's position. Bill would never try to challenge her because he knew if he displeased her, she needed only to make a single call to ruin him.

If my mom called the police, she'd say I had finally remembered who my rapist was. She'd demand a paternity test which would provide the evidence against Bill. The baby's parentage would be proven and charges would be pressed. This was a scenario that Bill would take any means possible to prevent from happening.

The Statue of Limitations varies from state to state, but most states offer a longer time for reporting statutory rape. In my state, there's no time limit for criminal rape. Of course, she would also press additional charges to include assault and battery; saying my refusal to identify Bill was because he had threatened me. However, in our beloved state of Texas, there's a 4 year limit when filing assault as a civil suit or a 2 year limit when filing under criminal. Regardless, my mom owned Bill and we all knew it.

The problem was that I didn't want her to own me and I sure as hell didn't want her to own my baby. I needed to figure out what I wanted to do and fast. With the way I was watched, it was going to be a challenge to try to implement any plan I came up with. More difficult was who I'd petition to help me and how. Sadly, I accepted that Dr. Maxwell would be my only knowing and willing collaborator.

I had little faith in the system helping me personally. They hadn't done anything to protect me so far and I didn't have any expectation that that would change any time soon. However, Dr. Maxwell was the one person who did believe me and who truly wanted to help me. Furthermore, he'd committed to helping me and I was counting on him not to let me down. He was my only hope for saving my baby.

I still had a lot to figure out, but I was comforted knowing that I was making headway. Though I knew there was no promise of success, I knew Dr. Maxwell's clout and coordination was my only chance. People would take him seriously and he had the pull to get them to agree with and participate in my crazy scheme.

I knew it was wrong, but I hoped his guilt would benefit me. I hoped he would feel so bad about not being able to help me out of my situation that he'd work that much harder to protect my unborn child from being trapped in it with me. Dr. Maxwell's complete allegiance was absolutely essential to me achieving my goal.

***

I didn't know what the future held in store for me. I was afraid as I walked into Dr. Maxwell's office. Normally, my mother or step-dad kept tight reigns on me and escorted me everywhere I went, but not today. Today was a unique day; a day when I was allowed to attend my doctor's appointment without supervision.

I knew that this amazing freedom was out of necessity. My mother and step-dad were meeting with Bill and their lawyers to cement their confidential agreement. Bill no longer came to our home and my parents only spoke to him through their lawyer. My mother wanted nothing to interfere with her gaining from my situation. That being said, she handled things the way she knew best; with extreme caution and ultimate control.

My mother worried that my step-dad would give away secrets, imagined or real. She no longer allowed him to be friends with Bill and forbade him to have any unauthorized contact. At first, my step-dad was happy to oblige, but as time went on, it wore on him. He missed his life-long friend and he grew bitter towards me the longer the separation continued.

I felt bad for him, but he was a grown man and I wasn't the one imposing the order. He could rectify the situation if he was so inclined. Of course, that would require him to grow a pair and I didn't see him having a sack of his own any time too soon. Even if he managed to find his balls, my mom's nuts were always going to be bigger.

I was kept in isolation as much as possible. My mother worried that Bill would get violent if he was left alone with me. She didn't want him to have access to me and potentially inflict harm on me that could result in a miscarriage. In learning that fact, I understood why her abusive behavior had halted. She'd do nothing to jeopardize this pregnancy.

I had no doubt that she would resume her old habits once the baby was born. I was even more convinced that the beatings would be worse than before. She'd need to make up for the lost time and God help me when she figured out what I planned to do with my child! I was sure that that would result in the worst beating of my life.

"Tiffany," Dr. Maxwell greeted me warmly. "How are you?"

"Fat," I smiled in return. He just chuckled.

"You look lovely and no ER visits," he noted. "And no parental supervision today, I see."

"Nope," I agreed. I neglected to add further comment on that issue. I took my seat and wasted no time in getting straight to my point, saying, "I need your help."

"You've decided on your course of action then," he guessed.

"I have," I confirmed. "You're still in, right?"

Dr. Maxwell looked intense and deeply concerned. "Of course, what can I do for you?"

"I want to put my baby up for adoption," I told him without hesitation.

"What?" he seemed surprised. "Are you sure?"

"Positive," I reaffirmed my stance.

"But your mother said..." Dr. Maxwell started and then stopped almost immediately. He looked chagrined and I just smiled at him patiently. "Sorry."

"It's cool," I reassured him. "She has that effect."

"Tiffany, there are other ways," Dr. Maxwell started. "It won't be long before you'll be eighteen and you can take your baby and leave. No one will be able to stop you."

"She will," I stated confidently.

"I'll help you," he reassured me.

"Help me with this," I replied. I could see his turmoil easily enough through his expression. I knew he didn't want things to end this way; he wanted me and my baby to have a chance together. I just knew that wasn't feasible.

"I can take you to a woman's shelter or-" he tried to change my mind, but it was already too late. This was the right way; the only way.

I interrupted him by saying, "I know, but how would I provide for my baby? I can barely take care of myself."

"There are programs in place to help you," he told me.

"And there are lawyers who'll fight on behalf of my mom or even Bill. There are lawyers who'll gladly help them take my baby away from me and maybe even get me committed."

"You don't know that," he tried to refute my words.

"I do know that and so do you," I asserted. "I also know that they'd have a good chance of winning custody based on my inability to provide a stable home and their existing relationships with the baby."

"Tiffany, I'll help you," he promised. "You don't have to do this. You can keep your baby."

I shook my head, "No, Dr. Maxwell. I don't want my baby to be a pawn in a sick game. I want my baby to have better than that."

Dr. Maxwell looked resigned. "What do you intend on doing?"

"I don't know how to make it all happen yet, but I don't want my mother in the delivery room. I want her to be told the baby died and I don't want anyone except us to know otherwise. I want someone in the delivery room that can take the baby out without detection and I want my baby placed for adoption."

"What about Bill?" the doctor questioned. "You just said he will have rights as the father."

"I won't name a father on the birth certificate. That should be enough and if he thinks the baby is dead then he can't contest anything. I want the adoption to be a closed adoption. I neither want my baby to be able to contact me nor us to find a way to contact the baby."

"That's going to be tricky," Dr. Maxwell said, but nodding in agreement he added, "I'll see what I can do."

"You have to do better than that. You *have* to make it happen."

I knew I looked desperate because I was desperate. I could see myself reflected in Dr. Maxwell's eyes and though I appreciated his concerns, I needed him to do this. As he looked at me, I knew he knew it too.

"I'll make it happen," he promised.

"Thank you," I said, relieved.

I knew I could trust Dr. Maxwell. He was always true to his word and though he seemed unable to help me get away from my mother, he did whatever he could to make life easier for me. My case would be hard to prove in a court of law and since I appeared in good health, had appropriate attire, nice accommodations, and a full belly, no one seemed concerned. I was old enough to fend for myself and there were others far worse off who needed attention. The fact my mother had stopped sending me to the emergency room helped too.

I knew Dr. Maxwell felt bad, but I understood. There's only so much a person can do and my mother was good. She knew how to play the game better than anyone. She was a force to be reckoned with; an act of nature. I knew how hard she fought so I didn't blame anyone who failed in their attempts to conquer her.

The best I could hope for was to outsmart her enough to keep my baby away from her. As long as my baby would be hidden from her in a closed adoption then I'd be satisfied. It hurt to think of giving up my baby, but I loved my baby enough to shoulder the pain. I didn't want my child to know it had been a product of rape and I didn't want it to be an instrument for my mother to use at her whim.

As I walked the short distance from the bus line to my house, I felt content. I was happy knowing things were being put into place in order to protect for my child. I was lost in thought, thinking about the potential life my baby could have, so I was unaware of his presence. He had been waiting by the back of house, waiting for me; he knew I'd be alone. When I unlocked the door and started to open it, Bill shoved me inside and latched the door behind us.

I was shocked and taken completely off guard. I hurled across the small expanse of the kitchen, stumbling into the table. I turned my shocked expression towards him and he laughed smugly. I felt sick looking at him and I was terrified when I realized that Bill had orchestrated today's events.

"Hi, Tiff-Tiff," he smirked, "Are you happy to see me?"

"What are you doing here?" I asked fearfully as I tried to navigate around the kitchen table so it was positioned between us.

"Oh, your step-daddy told me you had a doctor's appointment today," he looked at me, waiting to see my reaction.

"He's talked to you?" I asked in surprise.

"Oh, I'm sorry," Bill said feigning embarrassment for his faux pas. "That was a secret; I wasn't supposed to tell you."

Understanding dawned on me. My step-dad was lonely and he'd missed his childhood friend enough to disobey my mother's order to discontinue interactions with Bill. Apparently, my step-dad was feeding information about me, my pregnancy, and our schedules to his forlorn friend, just as my mom postulated. Bill had known my step-dad well enough to easily manipulate him in order to extract the desired information.

Bill must have realized that I had pieced things together from the look on my face because he said, "That man's so needy, isn't he? It's easy to get him to tell me what I want to know. I just have to stroke his ego a bit, like telling him how much he means to me."

I scoffed, "You don't care about him."

"Perhaps some praise to loosen his lips?" In a mockingly sweet voice he added, "I just want to do right by Tiffany because I want to be a good dad, like *you*."

"You're sick," I told him. He just shrugged at me indifferently.

It was easy for me to see how he'd planned my parent's absence in order to catch me alone. He could easily calculate and manipulate events based on the tidbits of data he'd received. He knew us all well enough to know our habits and to account for potential obstacles. Bill's plan had worked perfectly without any deviations and now I was at his mercy.

"What do you want?" I demanded.

"You know what I want," he answered as he made his way towards me.

I looked around for something to defend myself with; to defend my baby with. I dashed towards the cutlery set to grab a knife, but he rammed me before I could reach it. He crushed me between him and the counter, making me cry out. I was terrified; not for myself, but for the life of my unborn child. Bill was doing everything he could to try to direct damage to my abdomen.

"Stop," I begged. "You don't have to do this."

"Ah, but I do," he told me. "See, as long as that *thing* exists then your mother owns me."

Bill pulled me away from the counter and pushed me towards the living room. I stumbled as he handled me roughly. He backhanded me, knocking me to the ground then he kicked me violently in the side. I groaned and flinched away trying to move away from his raised foot as he prepared to stomp directly down on my stomach. Understanding his intention, I quickly scrambled aside, thwarting his efforts.

"Stop, please!" I cried. "I can handle this. I can make it stop, I promise."

"Bullshit," Bill spat at me. "You're nothing but a turd your mother shat out."

He lurched at me and I scampered awkwardly to the other side of the room. Frustrated, he roared and swatted at me. He just caught my arm, but I managed to break free of his grasp before he got a firm hold on me. My heart was racing and I tried for the front door.

Bill was faster. He came up behind me while I tried to unlock the bolt and crushed me in a bear hug from behind. "Let me go!" I screamed.

"You stupid bitch, it didn't have to be like this," he struggled to maintain his hold of me as I fought with all my might. "I was planning to just terminate the pregnancy, but now I'm really pissed off."

"Argh!" I screamed incoherently as I finally broke his hold on me and headed towards the back door.

I was afraid to look behind me; to know how close he was. It didn't matter because he tackled me before I made it to the kitchen. The air whooshed out of my body as I slammed into the ground and he landed with full force against me. I tried to scream for help, to tell him to stop, but I was struggling to regain my breath. There was no way I could speak.

He rolled me over as if I was a ragdoll and he punched me in the side of the head. I was immediately stunned and there was a ringing in my ear. My vision blurred and I felt like I was floating. My thoughts were confused, though I felt it when he lifted himself off me and kicked me violently again.

As I lay there trying to get my wits about me, I could hear him skittering about the kitchen; rummaging through the utensils. The sound was like thunder in my ears when I heard the knife slide out of its sheath. That motivated me to put more effort into my fight. I rolled over and started to crawl across the floor towards the front door in a hopeless retreat.

"Where do you think you're going?" he laughed wickedly. He kicked me in the ass with enough force to lurch me forward, causing me to slam my face into the floor as I collapsed.

"Help," I hollered weakly, desperately as I frantically tried to get up to continue forward. "Someone please help me."

"No one's going to help you. You know how I know?" he said as he yanked me up and back, partially lifting me off the ground by my hair. Getting very close to my ear he added, "Because you're nothing. No one gives a shit about you; you're forgettable and now, you're dead."

I saw the knife move in front of my face and I knew that Bill was going to cut my throat. I screamed out as my mother burst in through the back door. She and my step-dad were just arriving home from the lawyer's office and upon hearing my plea, they raced forward to find Bill laughing above me.

"You're too late," he said and I felt the blade glide across my skin.

Instinctively, I had thrown my hands up and shoved against his arm. I wasn't strong enough to stop him from cutting me, but my force had been enough to prevent him from killing me. The slice was only a surface wound, but it induced a lot of bleeding and stung like a son of a bitch.

"What have you done?!" my mother demanded from somewhere in the hazy distance.

"I've closed your bank account, you arrogant bitch," Bill cackled happily, cruelly.

"You bastard!" my mother screamed, running forward.

Bill dropped me to confront my mother's imminent attack. As he did, he lost his grip on the knife and it hit the floor beside me. My mother used my body to aid her in her assault and easily knocked Bill to the ground as they fell over me. I tried to scoot away from them as my step-dad's hand flashed across my line of vision. I thought he was reaching out to help me move, but he picked up the knife instead.

As I rolled away, curling up on my side and trying to apply pressure to my neck, Bill punched my mother away from him. As they broke apart, they both became aware of my step-dad. He was standing hesitantly with the knife raise in front of him in a defensive position.

"Stab him, damn it! Stab him!" my mother was yelling.

My step-dad looked uncertain. Bill laughed and said, "He won't kill me. Isn't that right, *friend*?" My step-dad just sort of blinked at them.

"Worthless," my mother said in exasperation.

In one smooth move, surprising everyone in the room, my mother yanked the knife from my step-dad's hand and thrust it into Bill. My step-dad issued a weird squawk, but Bill didn't have time to respond since he was taken completely off guard; he just looked shocked. He stared at my mom with wide eyes and made a choking sound, the knife sticking out of his throat. Looking him in the eye, my mom twisted the knife then withdrew it slightly before plunging it back into him. I knew my mom was making sure the job had been done thoroughly. She wanted to ensure she had caused as much damage as possible; ensuring Bill's demise.

Perhaps the events weren't as dramatic or as smooth as they seemed. I knew my perception was skewed, but it sure seemed like an incredible feat to me. I looked at my mother with a heightened sense of awareness. Though I was thankful for the end, I was terrified at the depth of violence she had hiding just below the surface. Though I was happy to see Bill die, I was acutely aware that my mother had killed him ruthlessly. I had no doubt in my mind that when the time came, she'd kill me just as easily.

That thought made me refocus on my present condition. If I died, my baby surely would and what if exsanguination occurred? What if I went into shock; how deeply had my throat really been cut? I could already feel myself slipping down a slope from which I wasn't sure I could return. I felt disconnected and I knew I had precious few minutes before my book of life closed for good.

Again, my mother surprised me. She turned and came to sit beside me. She replaced my hands, applying pressure to my wound as she barked orders to my step-dad. She told him to call 911 then my mother continued to talk to me, trying to keep me conscious. It was hard to stay lucid and I was afraid to talk, but I was conditioned to obey. My mom seemed okay with my lack of verbal responses as long as I stayed alert, focused on her.

The rest of the time was lost to me. I was weaving in and out of reality, dreams, and nothingness. I had moments of searing pain when my body was moved and I don't remember how I got to the hospital. I lost all sense of time and nothing seemed real in my crazy fog. At times I didn't know if I was still alive, but alive I was, thanks to my mother.

CHAPTER ELEVEN

You know, I used to think the worst feeling in the world was the sense of being hated. I thought perhaps it was potentially the negative emotion of hatred itself. Believe it or not, I was wrong; that's not the worst feeling.

Furthermore, the worst feeling isn't the pain of being hurt by someone holding you hostage. It's not the feeling of being trapped, powerless; unable to prevent your captor from doing things to you against your will. It's actually much simpler than that.

The worst feeling in the world is primal. It speaks volumes about a person and the shame a human can bare. The worst feeling in the world is losing your child and feeling happy you did.

After a whirlwind of activity and emergency care, I was on my way to recovery. Well, physical recovery anyway. I doubted I would ever get past the emotion damage I endured.

My physical treatment consisted of a procedure called a D&C. I was told that it is a medical procedure that is performed after a miscarriage. It stands for "Dilation and Curettage" and is used to ensure all the fetal material has been removed by scraping out the endometrium in order to prevent infection or excessive bleeding. With the trauma on my body, this was deemed necessary along with care for the gash across the side of my neck and some broken bones.

I had been very lucky that I'd been strong enough to thwart Bill's attempt at cutting my throat. Though I'd gotten a nasty slice, I'd prevented it from being deep enough to be fatal. It was more of a superficial wound than anything. Though the knife didn't go deep enough to knick my jugular veins or artery, it had made a bloody mess. I was certain that was the main reason Bill had not tried to repeat the action; the amount of bleeding made him feel satisfied that he'd done the job the first time. This was one situation where I was thankful that looks were deceiving.

I knew that the scars visible on the outside of my body would heal and fade. The doctors did a great job patching me up. Once I healed, most of my wounds would go unnoticed by people unless they took a closer look. Still, the unseen scars were the big concern. The emotional trauma and memories would haunt me forever.

I met with Dr. Maxwell twice a week in order to heal from the emotional trauma, but I wasn't sure it was doing any good. I struggled with the meaning behind my joy of losing my baby and having the father of said child murdered in front me. It made me question what sort of person I was and I was afraid to know the answer.

I searched for answers as to why my mother had acted the way she did. This woman who I knew hated me beyond all reason had acted to save my life; why? I wanted to believe it was because somewhere inside her, she loved me, but I couldn't seem to accept that on any level. I just couldn't see my mother having the ability to love anything more than she loved herself or the money she'd wanted.

Regardless of the intentions behind my mother's actions, I had to be grateful to her for what she did. Had she not acted as quickly as she did, I definitely would have died. It wasn't hard for me to comprehend that my mother had most likely acted out of anger, feeling personally insulted. That made more sense to me than thinking she'd acted on my behalf. Still, I was breathing because she came home, disarmed Bill, and called the ambulance in time. Just another reason I owed my mother; no doubt it would be something else she'd never let me forget.

Everything with my mother seemed bitter-sweet. There always seemed to be a price tag attached to everything; good and bad. My mom expected gifts without obligation though she never gave things freely herself. This was uncomfortable and upsetting for many reasons, but primarily it was because I never had a say in what she'd give or what she'd take in return. I lacked control in all aspects of our relationship.

I was in the hospital through the initial ruckus of the event. Thankfully, I missed all the news coverage and publicity. I missed all the chaos and craziness that followed the arrival of the medics and police. I wasn't immune to the questioning however and though I had only shady memories of how it all that went; I vaguely recalled several people asking me the same questions repeatedly. I knew my answers had remained consistent despite my haze.

Though my mother was initially arrested, she was released almost immediately into my step-dad's custody. This was due to friends at the police station who had helped to expedite her case so she could get to the hospital. They knew she ought to be with me and not in a cell. When all the evidence proved that she'd acted in self-defense, along with my step-dad and I corroborating her story, the case was quickly closed.

Despite my mother having her brief time in court, she didn't have to do any actual jail time. Based on the facts, the charges were dismissed as justifiable homicide. In our beloved state of Texas, there is a "duty to retreat", but that can be excused depending on the circumstances. If you can show that you had no other alternative in order to protect you or someone else, then you can claim justifiable homicide without penalty.

My mother's lawyers painted a convincing picture because it really was the truth in this case. The lawyers proved without a doubt that I would have died if my parents had both retreated from the scene. Bill surely would have ended my life and if my parent's had tried to carry me away, he was ruthless enough to attack one or both of them as well. Hence, the lawyers said my mom was faced with a "kill or be killed" scenario. In the end, the jury cleared my mother of all charges for reasons of self-defense.

Of course, it was an easy decision given the facts and considering Bill had caused the death of our child. Not only did the jurors sympathize with my mother, the media did as well. My mom was given all sorts of support, sympathy, and to her delight, gifts. After all, what parent wouldn't kill to save their child? It was bad enough my mom lost her grandchild and almost her daughter; no one wanted to take anything more from her, especially not her freedom!

In the end, no one seemed to even miss Bill. My mother missed his money and the potential of having some of it, but that was the only thing she seemed bothered by. Taking Bill's life hadn't fazed her in the least bit and she wasn't even sad about the baby, just the money the baby represented. I figured if I had died she'd have been just as unscathed. As a matter of fact, if I had died, it would have saved her a ton of money. With the mounting doctor bills, I was the object of her hatred once again.

I just couldn't do anything right. I couldn't live right and I sure as hell couldn't die right. Once again, my behavior and existence was detrimental to my mother. I made her life so hard to bear and she made sure everyone knew it. She milked the sympathy from anyone and everyone who'd listen. People fed into her story, keeping her happy through my initial recovery, but eventually public interest faded and so did her joy.

At first, people were aghast to hear how my mother lost her grandchild. They were sympathetic when she told them about the attempted murder of her daughter, me. Everyone cheered at her bravery in being able to kill my attacker herself. The injustice of almost being prosecuted for defending me was just shocking. People poured their concern onto my mom and she basked in the attention.

It amazed me how Bill's back story and involvement in our family changed. My mother painted a whole new picture of him to the press. Bill went from my step-dad's childhood friend to just some guy I brought home one day. Her story was that I had met him in a chat room on the internet and my parents, trying to protect me, allowed him to visit under their supervision. Of course, being the wild child that I was, I managed to get into trouble despite my parent's best efforts.

Unsurprisingly, even Tom, Silvia, Alice, and Molly were my mom's greatest supporters. They all had their 20 minutes of fame, being interviewed in and out of the courthouse. None of them admitted to being friends with Bill; they all added to my mother's fables, building a picture of the horrible person Bill had been. I was both fascinated and appalled by the ease with which most people seemed to be able to lie. It was amazing what people said and did when put in front of an audience.

Even people who knew that Bill had been a life-long friend of my step-dad wouldn't correct the popular stories being told. People seemed so willing to accept a lie despite all evidence that debunked it and even more willing to partake in the lie itself. Perhaps no one wanted to take blame or responsibility for letting bad things happen. Perhaps it was easier to just go along with whatever scheme my mother came up with than to acknowledge their involvement and hence, guilt for not stepping in sooner. I just didn't know.

I understood that no one wanted to admit being friends with someone like Bill, but that didn't change the truth. The truth wasn't that I was a juvenile delinquent who brought a killer home to screw; the truth was that Bill had been let into my home and life by my parents. Bill had been welcomed by them and their mutual friends. I tried to be forgiving, seeing them all as lonely, needy people who clung onto one another because they had no one else to turn to, but it was difficult. I really just found it all to be disgusting.

When that attention died away, it was gone as quickly as it had come. It left a hole in my mom's life that seemed bigger now than before and her need for the spot light was unfulfilled. This left her antsy, angry, and tense. Despite her few cronies who couldn't get enough of the tales mother told them, she was no longer the focus of our community or our local media. That left her searching for other outlets to fulfill her craving for attention.

When we were home alone, life was not very pleasant. My mother never let me forget the anguish I had caused her by losing the baby, by losing her money. As the doctor bills grew, so too did her animosity. The monetary gifts she'd been given had come and gone without a thought; not a penny had been spent on bills. Instead, she'd gotten a new wardrobe for the cameras.

My mother was constantly finding ways to "accidently" bump, poke, or stab my abdomen. When she did, she'd yell at me to stop being so clumsy, as though I were hitting her instead. She seemed to enjoy the way I cried out when she'd touch my tender belly or stroked a broken rib. Of course, I knew she'd eventually tire of this new game. Soon she'd need a bigger release and that would be when the beatings would commence again.

I dreaded the backlash that was coming. It was kind of her to wait long enough for me to heal, allowing me to be strong enough to withstand her punishments. That was so gener-ous of her. The torture I endured from her constantly touch-ing my wounds would be nothing in comparison to what she planned. Her hatred for me had grown exponentially. I just hoped my birthday arrived before her restraint ended.

The days were growing fewer and her patience was grow-ing thin. She was getting restless and more volatile. She was finding more things to be angry about and she seemed furious that I had physical restrictions that prevented me from doing all the chores she wanted to task me with. Yeah, it wouldn't be long before all hell broke loose.

"You're worthless," she told me over breakfast. "The one job you have in life – to bear a child – and you managed to fuck that up. What's wrong with you?"

"A poor excuse of a woman, that one," my step-dad piped in.

I didn't know what to say to her. I just sat quietly, avoiding eye contact. I hadn't missed this, this hostility. I wondered if it was really worse than I remembered or if it just seemed that way since I had had a reprieve from it for so long. It didn't really matter. I knew the break in abuse had only been temporary and that the rebound would be all the more dif-ficult for it.

"Look at me when I'm talking to you, whore," my mother ordered and stabbed me with her fork.

I yelped in pain as the fork punctured my flesh. My mother stopped moving, freezing in place. She stared at her fork as it protruded from my hand. After a minute, she burst into laughter.

Fortunately, the fork had landed on the meaty part of my hand between my thumb and index finger. My hand had been positioned just right as to avoid any real damage. My hand was curled into a loose grip as it rested on the table, pinky finger on the bottom. This left the fleshy area pointing upward and fully exposed for the assault.

I stared at the fork in disbelief, unsure what to do. Surprisingly, I didn't have a lot of pain after the initial piercing. I wasn't sure if that was because of the location or my shock. I began to feel really hot and woozy. I could hear my heart as it beat loudly in my ears and my body sort of tingled with prickles of energy.

My step-dad looked bewildered. He kept shifting his focus between my mom and me. He seemed as unsure about what to do as I was. Every now and then he'd expel a confused, irresolute chuckle.

As my mind started to glaze over with a weird foggy sensation, I tried to remember if it was better to leave the fork in place or to pull it out. Everything just seemed so unreal and I felt so disconnected. Was this really happening? Nawh; couldn't be. I mean, who actually stabbed someone in the hand with a fork?

My mother's laughter sounded distant and strange. I looked at her askance, trying to understand, as she got up and yanked the fork from my hand. My inquisitive expression must have looked rude because my mother abruptly stopped laughing when she looked directly at me. Before I knew it, she struck me in the face with a resounding *thwack*. I felt the sensation of falling before I felt the jerk as my body hit the ground and then nothing.

***

I knew that, yet again, my voice would not be heard. I understood that my status as a middle-class white girl about to turn eighteen, whose seemingly-caring parents escorted her to the ER, didn't scream for help. Even with red flags floating around us, I was a low priority for concern. There were children in much worse conditions who demanded the limited resources available more than I did.

I also realized that, thanks to my mother's prowess from previous visits, this trip to the ER would be considered another result of my mental health. Maybe it would be spun that my injuries were due to the company I kept, with Bill being a shining example. Of course, I wasn't disappointed in my expectations. My mother gave her account of how I got a fork embedded in my hand and no one questioned it.

I was processed through the ER in no time at all. Everyone sympathized with my mother, and I was quickly patched up under reproachful eyes. I didn't bother trying to explain much, especially since the only explanation anyone wanted to hear was the entertaining fiction my mother was spewing. She could put on a good show; I'd give her that.

"We were having a lovely breakfast and then she just came unhinged," my mother told the doctor and his nurse.

The doctor was shaking his head in disapproval while the nurse *tsked*, clicking her tongue in contempt. I rolled my eyes, but thankfully, no one noticed. My lip was swollen from the impact of my mother smacking me. She explained it away as a result of my hitting the floor when I passed out. My face was throbbing, as was my hand. Being right-handed, I was at least thankful that it was my left hand which she'd stuck with the fork.

"It must be the people she's hanging out with. They live on the streets and they're teaching her these awful things," my mother said all flustered. "I bet you see this kind of thing all the time."

"Yes, we see a lot of crazy things here," the doctor concurred.

"You wouldn't believe what some people do and the stories they tell to explain them is just unbelievable," the nurse said. If only she knew how true those words were.

Ugh, if only there was some way I could make people see the truth. If I could catch it on camera – inspiration! If I could manage to purchase a camcorder and get her on film then they'd have to listen to me, right? I mean, film footage would be undisputable evidence. I could prove once and for all that I was not crazy and that she was an abusive she-demon. Why hadn't I thought of that before?

The nurse was passing my mother some tissue when I refocused on their exchange. "You poor dear," the nurse said.

The doctor had left the curtained off section that was my "room" and I wondered how I'd missed him go. My mother blubbered louder and said, "Why would she be so self-destructive? We do everything for her; we give her attention and tell her how beautiful she is. I don't know what we're doing wrong?"

"There, there, honey," my step-dad stood and moved beside her, patting her on the back in a consoling way.

"Oh, sweetie, you mustn't blame yourself," the nurse said. "You can only do so much. At some point children need to grow up and take responsibility for themselves." She looked at me then and added, "You should be ashamed; look at what you're doing to your folks."

Oh, puke, puke, choke, gag; really? Yeah, I definitely wanted to get a camcorder and when I did, this nurse would be the first one I showed it to! I couldn't believe how people just soaked up my mother's shit. I just wanted to scream, but I held myself in check. I didn't want to make a bad situation worse.

The doctor returned then with two police officers in tow. The doctor looked embarrassed when he explained, "I know you've been through a lot already and I'm sorry, but procedure mandates that we call the police in a situation like this."

"No, no, we understand," my mother wept. "There's no need to feel bad. We have nothing to hide."

"Of course, you don't," the doctor replied, patting my mother on the back.

"We appreciate your understanding and cooperation," one of the police officers said.

I lost focus again as my mother rehashed the morning's alleged events to the authorities. Though the first officer seemed to be buying the story my mother was selling, the second officer was watching me carefully. I returned his look with my own dull, empty expression. I wanted to challenge him to do something, anything, but I just gave up before I even mustered the energy to finish the thought.

Bored with the drama and my parents sickening display, I curled up on the gurney and rolled into a little ball on my side. I pulled the sheet over my head and cradled my sore hand to my chest. The throbbing was excruciating, but the pain pills were kicking in, taking the edge off. I didn't know how long we'd be here or even if I'd be let out this time. Seeing as I was crazy, I'd probably land myself back in the hospital's mental ward. I sighed.

I heard movement and I peeked out from under the sheet I had covering my head. The police officer was still watching me; creepy. The doctor had left and the nurse explained that as long as my parents felt safe, I could return home with them, but under strict supervision. My mother immediately refused custody of me, exclaiming that she feared for her life. I shook my head slightly before I recovered my face. At least the creepy watcher cop didn't appear convinced by her statement; not that it mattered when push came to shove.

As soon as my mother said she was worried I'd hurt her or my step-dad, my fate was sealed. Arrangements were swiftly made and I was promptly shipped off to the mental ward. I was getting somewhat used to the new practice and I even recognized some of the nursing staff; some of the other patients even. That familiarity was actually comforting and somehow made things easier on me.

Screw my mom. She may have thought she was getting a break from me and building her story up about my insanity, but I didn't care. I was getting a vacation from her and a safe haven in which to sleep soundly, for a change. She thought she was so smart; *humph.* The mental ward wasn't the hell she figured it to be; it was practically a vacation spa compared to home.

While I was locked up yet again, I worked on my plans to show the world my mother's true face. I plotted my steps for securing a camera and ways in which I hoped I could film my mother in action. I'd see an end to this madness once and for all. Finally, I'd be vindicated, proving my side of the story. "A picture is worth a thousand words," the saying goes, so how many is a video worth? I couldn't wait to find out!

When I met with Dr. Maxwell later that week, I told him what I was planning to do. He was excited by the idea of getting concrete evidence of the real situation I lived in, but he seemed nervous. He was very cautious and didn't seem to want to give me much advice. The doctor was leery and he appeared hesitant, not wanting to encourage my excitement in case things didn't work out.

I understood his stance, but I was hopeful despite everything. This was the first time in a long time that I felt like I had a real chance to change things. I understood that it was going to be a tricky process and I fretted over details, wondering how I'd manage the feat. How would I catch her on film when I never knew what was coming or when? Regardless of the obstacles I might face, I couldn't help my optimism.

CHAPTER TWELVE

"The neighbors told me they saw you in a car with a boy," my mother began. She wanted to see whether I'd lie to her about it; whether I'd say the neighbors were wrong.

They weren't wrong and I refused to lie about helping a friend, so I said, "Angie was there too and I sat in the backseat - alone."

"They said he was a *black* boy," my mother pursed her lips.

"So?" I questioned, "Does that matter?" I knew it did. My mother was an incredibly racist and bigoted.

"You know it does," she said with disdain.

"To them or to you?" I pressed. I knew I was treading on dangerous ground, but I couldn't help myself; I had little tolerance for blatant ignorance, even from my mother. I didn't care whether she beat me or not, I needed to stand up against her prejudice.

I never understood the concept of racism. To me, we were all the same and skin color was no different than say, eye color or hair color. We're all the same animal when it comes down to it: Homo sapiens. We needed to get over our stupidity and just accept one another. We needed to stop the process of classification and quit trying to fit everyone and everything into little boxes. The only thing that should matter and the only title we should all be labeled is "Earthlings."

To be fair to my mother, I knew she'd have been pissed enough that I'd gotten into a car with my friend, Angie, let alone into a car with a boy. The fact that the boy had been African-American had only escalated the offense in her estimation. The neighbors witnessing the occurrence and then commenting to her about it merely sealed my fate. You've got to love a gossip.

In an attempt to appease my mother and save myself from her wrath, I explained further. I told her, "Angie and I were talking to him at the end of class because we're doing a project in government today."

"How's that explain anything, Tiffany?" my mother was getting worked up.

"Our government class is the last class of the day and the bell rang during our conversation about our final class project. We hadn't noticed the bell or the time because the project is a really big deal; it's like 20% of our overall grade."

She rolled her hand at the wrist. She was gesturing for me to hurry up with my explanation. Her agitation was increasing, but my explanation was satisfactory thus far, keeping her anger at bay. This fact was at least encouraging.

"Well, when we did realize the time, we all continued talking as we walked out to where the buses are lined up. When we got to where Cedric's bus was, it had already left. Angie drives to school, as you know, so she offered to take him home."

"And how does that in any way involve you?" My mother was fuming, but still listening. It was a rare feat to get to tell my side of a story and I was going to try to use it to my advantage. I wanted to save myself from punishment for something that was completely innocent.

"Well, it wouldn't be right to have Angie in a car alone with a boy, would it?" I asked in exaggerated innocence. My mother narrowed her eyes at me, but kept her mouth clamped tightly closed. "I told her that I'd ride with her to take Cedric home so her parents wouldn't be upset about it."

My mother was struggling to restrain herself. She so wanted to be punish me, but I had a valid argument and was playing the game with skill of my own. If she said I had been wrong to do it then it'd prove contrary to her ideals of a young female being alone in a car with a boy – a black boy to boot. I suppressed my own glee, though I thought, "Suck on that, you miserable hag!"

"You should have called me or let me know," she tried to find a new way to attack me. She wanted retribution for her embarrassment and an outlet for her growing frustration.

"I couldn't call you because I don't have a cell, but we did stop here, at home, first which is probably how the neighbors know about it," I continued. "I wanted to check with you first, but you weren't home."

"So you decided to go anyway?" my mom seemed excited; she saw a foothold to launch her attack.

"No, ma'am," I told her in mock surprise, "I'd never do that. I asked dad."

My mom was caught; I saw the surprise in her expression. "And he gave you permission?" she inquired cautiously.

"Yes," I said simply, batting my wide eyes innocently. Not only had my mother been unaware of the event, she'd lost the game; her foothold crumbled beneath her feet.

My mother was fit to be tied. It was fantastic to see her stuck in a winless situation; winless for her at least. Served her right, the old bat. How dare she hold herself above other people, especially people I knew to be better than her, even on their worst day?

Cedric was a great guy. He was funny and intelligent, handsome too. I'd known him since our freshman year and liked him from the moment we met. He was charming and honest. Cedric and I even worked together, but I wasn't going to remind my mother of that fact. I cared for Cedric and I didn't want her to push him from my life.

I considered myself color blind. I didn't care whether a person was black, white, purple, green, or spotted. If you were a good person then that was all that mattered to me. I knew a lot of people, people in all walks of life, but I only had a few real friends. Angie and Cedric were at the top of that very short list.

I never talked to them about my family and the abuse I sustained, though I knew they suspected things. How much they knew or inferred didn't matter because they loved me as I was and I loved them in return. We never expected anything more or less than what we had in the moment. Our time wasn't passed pissing and moaning about bad situations, but rather, celebrating in our friendship. My time with them was the only time I was ever truly happy.

I think if life had been different, I would have pursued my feelings for Cedric; we'd have been together. It was more than just our friendship that drew me to him. It was deeper than his beautiful mocha skin and chocolate eyes; it was his character. Cedric was chivalrous and kind, sincere and reliable. He was a dream come true.

There are some people in life that you immediately think are beautiful. Sometimes those people prove you right and they *are* beautiful, inside and out. Other times, they show their true nature and the beauty you initially saw disappears forever. Then there are the swans and butterflies of the world. Those are the people you thought were unappealing only to discover their true person, a person more beautiful than you ever knew.

I think the old adage that "beauty is only skin deep" is wrong because it's not complete enough. It's also misleading because "skin deep" sort of implies or gives the idea that beauty comes from outside. In my estimation, beauty is something that is radiated from *inside* the person. When a person can touch your soul, you always see them in a new way; one that transcends the physical. Perhaps I'm more of a "beauty is in the eye of the beholder" person. At any rate, Cedric was the stuff that defined beauty at its most perfect.

I could truly be myself with Cedric and he was always open and direct in return. I loved his laugh and the wrinkles around his eyes when he smiled; his smiles always reached his eyes and made them simply light up. I felt an easy acceptance both with and for Cedric. We could talk about anything and I knew I could confide in him, but I didn't; not about home anyway.

I didn't want to drag Cedric into the world I hid. He deserved more than that crap and I didn't want to tarnish our relationship with ugliness. I only wanted him to have joy when we were together, so we shared our love of music, literature, movies, and life. I felt truly alive when we were together and that endeared him to me all the more.

"I see I'm going to have to have a talk with your step-dad when he gets home," my mother stormed.

"Mom," I knew I should shut up and let this pass, but I wanted to hold her accountable. I wanted to defend my friends and my right to have the life I wanted and not conform to what other's chose for me. "Why do you care so much what the neighbor's think?"

My mother actually gasped. It was a small gasp, but I heard it; I reveled in it. "What?" she asked as though she couldn't believe I'd have the audacity to question anything she did or thought.

"I'm just saying, we know the truth and it's our business. It shouldn't matter to us what anyone else thinks or feels, right? Besides, don't they have their own affairs to manage; why're they so interested in ours?"

If my mother's stare could have burned me, it would have. Oh, she was furious! For a moment, I seriously thought my mother's head might burst. As she worked to stay calm, her coloring changed about five times. I would have laughed heartily if my instincts hadn't protected me. The danger light was blinking madly and I realized I needed to back away now.

"Sorry," I told her as I tried to defuse the situation. "I was just curious. I guess I still have a lot to learn about life and people." I blinked at her softly, trying to convey naivety.

My mother inhaled sharply through her nose, keeping her mouth locked shut. Her tightly-pursed lips made me think of a sphincter. I couldn't suppress my smile when I realized that, in my head, I had just called my mother a "butt face." In an attempt to save myself from hitting her detonation button, I had to cover the smile.

"I'm glad you're watching out for me and our family," I beamed. I was proud of myself that I had managed to say it without the sarcasm I felt. I sounded believable even to my own ears.

My mother had reached her boiling point. She huffed at me and clenched her fists, but then she abruptly turned and stomped out of the room. I stood in her wake feeling energized and joyful. I was in awe of the courage I had displayed and the skill with which I'd been able to confront my mother without repercussions. Wow.

***

I had to be sneaky. My mother had her little spies everywhere, ready to report any unusual activity I might pursue. It was sad really. I was a good student, an obedient daughter, and really too afraid of the consequences to allow myself to explore life to any degree. Truly, there was no need for her to have watch dogs on the job.

Today was the day I'd get the camera. Today was the day that I'd change the path my life was taking and direct it to a road I preferred. I wouldn't have to wait until I was a legal adult; I could have it now. All I had to do was to prove my case and break the spell my mother had the world under. I could do that.

I had been saving my money up for a long time. Whenever I got paid at work, my mother made me put it into an envelope that remained locked in her room. She kept it in a small, blue, waterproof and fireproof safe. Of course, I was neither allowed into her room nor told the whereabouts of the safe's key. For that reason, I had to lie. I wasn't proud of myself for doing it, but it was a necessity.

I'd always take a small amount from each paycheck after cashing it. I'd explain the money missing by telling my mother that I'd treated myself to lunch or put gas in the car; something she'd trust without question. I usually picked something that sounded selfish and something you couldn't really check into. That not only protected me from discovery, but it also delighted my mom, giving her a chance to yell at me.

When I did pick something traceable, like putting fuel into the gas tank of the car, I literally did. I'd put enough in to be near what I said, though I'd always stop short. For instance, if I said I'd gotten $10 worth of fuel then I'd only put in $8.50, pocketing the rest. To make that hidden savings larger, I'd also tell her that I'd grabbed a coke and snack as well. Of course, I never did buy the extraneous things I claimed; I squirreled the money away instead.

I barely slept the night before I was fixing to carry out my plan because I worried over details of my cover story. I'd told my mother that I had to stay after school for some tutoring because of something I'd missed while I was in the hospital. It was a legitimate cover because I truly needed to speak to my teacher about some of the details of my make-up work, but I wasn't actually being tutored. Also, I wasn't going to stay at the school.

As far as digital equipment went, I didn't need anything really fancy, just functional. I didn't have a lot of time so I had to be sure I went somewhere that had what I was looking for. I bought a cheap camera with a recording feature; actual camcorders were too pricey for me. It'd been refurbished so that helped to make it cheaper.

One concern I had was my mother snooping around and actually finding the camera. I hoped that seeing a camera instead of a camcorder would throw her off the scent; good camouflage for what its intended purpose was, I thought. I hoped; I hoped she wouldn't find it at all.

Though I was terrified that someone would see me and alert my mother, I felt a sense of peace when I held the camera in my hands. This little piece of technology was going to free me. The camera was worth so much more than the price I paid for it. It was a treasure beyond all others and it represented my pardon in life.

When I got home, my heart thudded in my chest. Though I knew my parents were both still at work, I was relieved to see that they were still gone. I had successfully planned this trip to coordinate with everyone's schedules, but I had to hurry. My seclusion wouldn't last for long.

I brought the camera into my bedroom and tucked it into a pile of stuffed animals on top of my dresser. There was no need to turn it on now, but soon I would. A shiver of anticipation ran through my body. I couldn't be sure what caused the shiver; it might have been fear, from knowing why I'd be turning it on, or pleasure, in finally having concrete evidence. It didn't really matter why because either way, there was light at the end of the tunnel.

CHAPTER THIRTEEN

"I hate you," my mother's voice dripped like venom. Still, this wasn't news to me.

"I know," I said simply, calmly.

"What?" my mother asked, surprised not only at my response, but that I actually had the audacity to have a response.

"I know you hate me," I told her matter-of-factly. "I've always known."

My mother's mouth hung slightly open. Did I really shock her into silence? My mother speechless - that was new. When she realized her mouth was hanging slightly open, she closed it, making a weird sound as she did. She quickly regained her composure, but I wasn't done shocking her yet.

"I hate you, too," I told her plainly.

"How dare you!" she spat.

"You aren't the only one allowed to have feelings, mother."

My mother actually looked stunned. I realized she was at a loss for how to respond to me. Her body twitched and her face contorted as she tried to decide whether she wanted to yell, lash out at me, or just remain immobile. I was fascinated as I watched her struggle with the fact that I actually had the will to stand up to her. What would more honesty do to her?

"I'm not afraid of you anymore," I informed her.

For a brief moment, my mother deflated. It was true; when you stood up to a bully, they'd just back down. Wait! Not true, not true! I saw the rage as it slowly filled my mother; replacing her shock with anger. My mother attacked me without further delay or warning.

At first, I did a decent job of protecting myself. I didn't try to strike my mother, but rather I worked to block her from landing any of the punches she dealt. My mother was furious that I didn't just accept her punishment. Her temper was inflamed by my attempts to dodge her beating. She called to my step-dad for assistance.

He came at a slight run and when he realized what was happening, he quickly jumped into the mix. My step-dad was able to catch me off guard enough to seize me. He locked my arms behind my back and tried to subdue my thrashing. With my attention now on trying to break free from my step-dad, my mother was clear to pounce. She struck me in the stomach with a few quick jabs.

Of course she'd go for my stomach; strategically, it was her best move. I was still recovering from the trauma of Bill's attack; she'd be able to cause considerable pain while hiding any additional damage. Any potential marks would be masked by the old wounds. As she suspected, it completely dropped my defenses and exposed me. My vulnerability was intoxicating to her.

As the breath left my body in a rush from the blows to my abdomen, I had a moment of stillness. My body sagged a bit and my head lurched forward slightly. This gave my mother a perfect shot which she took gladly. She reared back and slammed her hand across my face; her palm was held flat and her rings had been turned so that the stones would connect with the soft tissue of my face. I knew that the rings had been deliberately turned so that my mother could inflict the most amount of pain possible. She hit me again and again.

My mother enjoyed expending her anger. Once she saw that my face was no longer welting, but was actually cut enough to cause me to bleed on her floors, she changed things up. She opted to kick my shins, but thankfully she avoided my abdomen. I was grateful for that because I still felt dazed from her previous blows to my stomach, on the edge of throwing up. I knew I'd have hit the ground already if my step-dad hadn't continued to hold me steady.

My mother began to slow her actions and when she accidently kicked my step-dad instead of me, she stopped all together. He cried out and she started to laugh. It was a sickening sound, but it meant her anger had finally passed. My step-dad released me so he could check his leg, inspecting where my mother had made contact. I sank to the floor; my vision blurred with tears; my head swimming and my ears ringing.

"Damn, that hurt," my step-dad complained.

"Sorry," my mother laughed without remorse.

"I can already tell that's going to bruise."

"Stop belly-aching," my mother snapped at him. "You're fine."

"Yeah, but she's not," my step-dad pointed out.

"What?" my mother demanded to know.

My step-dad looked a bit uncertain for a moment. I wasn't sure I understood his hesitation. I wasn't sure if he was hesitant about acknowledging my need for care or was afraid my mother would turn her anger towards him for saying I needed help? At least I felt sure he knew the volatile my mother was. At least he managed to be concerned enough to see that I needed medical attention.

"I think she's going to need stitches, sweetie," he answered gingerly.

This made my mother take closer note of the damage done to my face. She reached to grab my chin tightly in her hand then she jerked my head around a bit as she inspected me. In disgust, she shoved me backwards with the hand crushing my jaw and huffed loudly in exasperation. Apparently, I couldn't even take a beating correctly.

"Shit!" she exclaimed. "I think you're right. Damn it."

I wanted to smile. I was happy knowing that at the very least she'd have a doctor's bill to pay for what she'd done. I had little faith that anything else would transpire, as history had proven that my mother was above reproach. She never received punishment for her crimes; never. Still, the monetary consequences were a small triumph that gave me a sense of joy.

I kept a tight hold of myself. I kept my eyes averted from my mother and I stayed silent. I knew my mother wasn't above losing her temper again and resuming the beating. I knew she wasn't above killing me. However, the new insight was the realization that my step-dad was not only capable, but willing to help her do it. He really would do anything to stay in her good graces; sick. Maybe he feared her as much as he loved her? I'd have to explore that idea at another time.

"Clean this fucking place up," my mother ordered my step-dad. "I guess I have to take dumbass to the ER."

"Don't worry about a thing, darling," my step-dad said as he jumped into action. "I'll take care of everything. It'll be just how you like it."

My mother rolled her eyes in irritation, but she seemed resolute. She left the room to go wash up a bit and to change her shirt; she wanted to remove any trace of her involvement in my appearance, including her rings. I wasn't sure what I was supposed to do while I waited, struggling to stay on my feet. I feared doing anything to agitate the situation and cause the beating to recommence. I was scared to move and I was scared to stand still.

When my mother returned, I noticed she'd grabbed her purse and keys. She paused a moment as though she expected something from me, but I was oblivious as to what that something was. Impatiently, she snapped her fingers a couple times in front of her, gesturing towards the door. Still, I didn't comprehend what she wanted, so I neglected to comply.

"Move!" she snapped at me as though she were talking to a dog, "Move." With that, she started to push me towards the door.

***

On our way to the emergency room, the drive was uneventful. We both kept to ourselves, avoiding all conversation save for a few moments of road rage and hostile gestures on my mother's part. She'd sung along to the radio while I slumped in the passenger seat, lost in my own thoughts. Though I had been successful in acquiring a video-capable camera and I'd anticipated a chance to use it to catch my mother in action, I didn't feel like a winner. I felt miserable.

I tried to get the recording to bring with us, ending this nightmare for good, but I'd been too stunned to remember to collect it, not to mention scared. Being in the broken state that I was, I just felt numb and my brain barely hummed with activity. However, even in my stupor, I recognized the spark of excitement. That excitement built as I recovered my strength and state of mind. I didn't know what I had caught on film, but the audio should be enough. I would finally be able to prove my story to the world.

When we entered the emergency room, all eyes were upon us. My mother knew how to work the system, so we were quickly ushered into the back. I was thankful that we'd gotten away from the waiting room and the staring faces so quickly that I tried not to be negative about my mother's manipulations. When we were closed off in the little curtained space, my mother prepared herself for the scene.

"What happened?" the nurse was asking her. No one had spoken to me directly since we arrived. My mom knew these people and they had a history with us. None of them would acknowledge me without my mom's say-so.

"I'm not sure," my mother began. "Tiffany went out to meet some friends and when she got home her face was this bloody mess!"

"Really?" the nurse remarked.

"You know the type of people she's been hanging out with lately," my mother said with disappointment and a touch of sadness. "They're not a good influence and they're all trouble makers."

The nurse nodded in understanding and acknowledgment. "So you think Tiffany got into an altercation with one or more of the people she met up with?"

"Must have, but she wouldn't tell me," my mother said in a disgruntled voice. "She said she'd only stopped home to get cleaned up a bit before she headed out to some party. When I tried to ask her about her face and the party, she got angry."

"Were her so-called 'friends' going to be at this party, too?" the nurse questioned and it was obvious by the tone of her voice that she was displeased with my imaginary friends, the fictitious party, and my dismissive behavior.

"Yes, they were," My mother affirmed. "Tiffany seemed hell-bent on getting even with them too."

"I bet," the nurse said.

"I told Tiffany there was no way in hell I was going to let her go to some random party. I said it'd have been different had the host's parents called me directly and confirmed they'd be supervising the party, but that hadn't happened."

"Uh-huh," the nurse was listening intently, occasionally typing notes into the small bedside computer.

"Even if it had, given the condition of her face, I wasn't going to let her go anywhere!"

"Right," the nurse said approvingly. "Good call."

"Oh, Tiffany got irate when I told her the only place she'd be going was here," my mother started.

"Of course," the nurse remarked as she took my vitals.

"I was afraid of what she'd do given her past, but I was firm in telling her no," my mother continued. "She needs structure and consequences."

"Exactly," the nurse said in support and encouragement. "There'd be fewer kids in here if more parents were like you."

"That's very sweet of you to say; thank you," my mother smiled in false modesty.

"No, thank you," the nurse replied. "If more parents said no and put stronger limitations in place then the world would be a better place."

"You're too kind," my mother beamed. "It's a challenge, but I know Tiffany needs it in order to learn to control her urges. I just don't know what to do about her nasty temper. As it was, Tiffany got so mad that she started to kick the coffee table. She said she'd keep doing it until I said she could go."

"Oh my," the nurse said as she did a quick examination of my shins.

My mother was in full story-telling mode. Having an avid listener just made her performance more heartfelt. "I told her to stop, saying she'd only hurt herself worse, but she said it didn't matter. She said she was fixing to tell everyone that I did it to her unless I let her go."

I rolled my eyes, but remained silent. What was the use in speaking? My voice was on mute anyway, so I just tried to act like I wasn't even there. The only person in my world with a microphone was my mother and she was in full command of her audience. She was riveting.

"I asked her why she'd do such a thing and she said it was because she hated me!" At this point, my mother burst into tears.

The nurse stopped what she was doing to attend to my frail mother. "There, there," she cooed, hugging my distraught mom as the doctor walked in.

"Can you believe she'd blame me?" my mother asked through a new wave of tears. "I just don't understand why she hates me so much. I try to do everything right; I give her everything I can, but it's never enough."

I observed her without emotion. Wow, she was good. She really deserved an award for her performance. "And the academy award goes to –." Yeah, she'll get something when I show them the footage of what really happened!

"Well, it's obvious your daughter has a history of mental health problems," the doctor told her. "It's just good that you were able to calm her down and reduce her violent behavior before she could do more damage."

"It was so scary," my mother expressed. "I've never seen anyone be so self-abusive. I felt so helpless. I mean, what am I supposed to do in a situation like that?"

Blah, blah, blah. I wanted her to stop talking. I wanted to yell at her to go back to the hole she had crawled out of. I felt a twinge of excitement when I thought about my recording; I'd be sure to send a copy to these fools. I wondered if the police actually *could* send my mother to a hole; how great would that be? I could almost sing, I was so light with happiness thinking about it. I'd finally unmask my mom, exposing the monster she really was. My anticipation for redemption made the pain bearable.

My subdued nature and weakened state made the medical staff agree to send me home with my mother. She said she was sure she could manage me, especially with the painkillers that were sedating me. The doctor warned her not to hesitate to call the authorities if I showed any signs of violence again. My mother was all charm and appreciation.

I tried not to seem smug or excited during our journey home. I just felt so good that this nightmare was going to be brought to light, that I was almost euphoric. This happiness carried me through the insults my mother threw at me during her reiteration of the evening's ER visit to my step-dad. It encouraged me to endure the drama until I was finally excused to my room. I tried not to run, but I headed straight for my little camera. As I stood there, trying to view the film, my mother came up behind me.

"What are you doing, Tiffany?" she asked confidently, scaring the crap out of me.

After I jumped about a foot and a half into the air, I said, "nothing."

"Damn, right," she replied triumphantly. "You got *nothing*."

She laughed as I realized the batteries had been removed from the camera. I felt completely defeated. How had she known?

"I found your fucking camera when I was looking through your shit the other day," she explained. "Why do you have a camera, huh?"

"She's probably going to make a sex video," my step-dad hollered, snorting.

My mother came across the room and, looking me straight in the eye, she said, "You'll *never* win." She said each word deliberately and precisely. "I *own* you." Then she shoved me away, propelling me backwards.

Both of my parents chortled loudly, thoroughly entertained. My mother tore the camera from my hands and slammed it against the top of the dresser I had crashed into. The action effectively cracked the lens. She smiled while she examined her work.

"Perfect," she said happily. "Let's see what you can do with this camera now."

My mother dropped the device into my lap and turned her back on me. As my parents walked off to do whatever it was that bat shit crazy people did, I just pulled into myself. I was deflated, devastated. I'd put so much hope into the camera, never taking into consideration that my mother might find it and guess its purpose. I hadn't thought she would understand my intentions, since I had the camera and not a camcorder.

It was stupid for me to have underestimated my mother. She was too good for me to have assumed her to be naïve about the camera's purpose. Furthermore, I knew she checked my room regularly; thoroughly taking stock of my possessions. I thought I'd been so careful, but my mother's words felt heavy on me and in that moment I agreed with her; I was stupid.

CHAPTER FOURTEEN

I didn't know what was happening, but I could feel it buzzing in the air around me. At first, I thought it was because I was nearing my eighteenth birthday and subsequently graduation. I was nearing the end of the line and about to take control of my life. That was reason enough to have an air of excitement, indeed, but it felt like there was more to it.

As time went on, I started to focus more on the subtle changes I was noticing, albeit feeling. Whatever it was seemed to be bigger than me; more than just my own growing anticipation. It felt darker than the joy of the landmark I was about to reach in life. It felt heavy and malicious, making me uneasy.

My mother had kept herself in check since I'd been stabbed by Bill. She was literally forced to refrain from physically punishing me. The night she had lost her grip and let herself lash out at me had set me back in my progress, but it hadn't ruined me. Still, it had taken its toll on my health, so my mother was once again forced to try to control herself. She was not pleased with this at all.

The way she eyed me was uncomfortable in itself. The way she watched my every move was sort of creepy. I thought it was just because she was unable to get the emotional and physical release she seemed to achieve from beating me, but it didn't really seem to fit. I was missing something; something vital. Whatever was happening seemed to be hinged on this missing factor.

"You think you're so grown," my mother hissed from my open bedroom door.

I had been sitting at my desk working on my homework. I thought it was weird that teachers still felt it necessary to give graduating seniors so much homework, but I supposed they wanted to keep us in practice. I eased my concern by deciding it was their way of preparing us for the amount of work we'd face in college. Thinking of it in those terms helped me to be less annoyed.

I planned to attend college. Despite wanting to be away from my mother, I couldn't afford out-of-state tuition. I had received a scholarship for Texas State University, so I decided to go there. The University was a few hours away from my mother's, so I'd be moving into the dorms. I was so excited when I received my acceptance letter. My acceptance letter! That was it; the thing I was missing. My acceptance into college had been the thing that brought about the change in me, my mother, and my home.

"You think you can do whatever you want now," my mother was in a tiff, though I wasn't sure why. "Don't think I haven't noticed your behavior lately, missy."

"What?" I was perplexed; what behavior was she referring to?

"You think you're such a hot shot," my mother sneered at me.

"I'm sorry," I told her, looking up from my desk confused. "I'm not sure what you mean?"

"You know exactly what I mean," my mother snapped. She grabbed a handful of my hair and wound it in her fist tightly. I squeaked a little in surprise and pain. "I won't tolerate your attitude."

I looked into her eyes with fright and barely squeaked out, "yes, ma'am."

"You think you're better than me, but you're not! Don't forget that you'd have nothing if it weren't for me," my mother spat the words out, actually getting some of her spittle on my face.

My mom shoved me away from her, causing me to slam my shoulder into the wall beside me. She looked at her hand and then wiped it off on her jeans as though she'd touched something that left a residue on her. I avoided eye contact, unsure where this hostility had come from, since I'd come straight to my room upon arriving home from school.

"Your dorm assignment came in the mail today," my mom informed me, tossing the opened letter on the desk in front of me.

I felt really excited, but I fought to contain my emotions. I realized that my mother was angry because she'd found the letter in the mail today. It never really took much to get my mom in a tiff, but this particular subject was a source of great resentment. My mom had never attended college because she was a single mother, so she saw my acceptance into college as a personal insult.

My mom had worked hard to get where she was in life and in her career. Her work ethic was incredible and something I admired in her character. She was a strong, intelligent woman capable of so many things. Her natural inclination for business served her well and the dedication she had to her work and company allowed her to prosper.

After I was born, my mom had started working as a supply clerk in the warehouse of a big oil and gas company in Houston. The pay and benefits were outstanding for an unskilled labor position and her personality allowed her to thrive in the field. She worked her way up, learning as much as she could about her business and ultimately became a buyer for the company. My mom had reason to be proud of her achievements, but she never was. In her eyes, the achievements made by others, including me, always lessened her own.

My mother had raised me with the expectation that I would attend college. She stressed the importance of an education and made it clear that she expected me to get at least a Bachelor's Degree. Though my mother wanted me to have better than she had, she still resented me. She blamed me for her inability to attend college and she resented me for having options that she had never had.

I knew that there was no way to win this struggle. It was filled with contradictions and double-edged swords, as were all things concerning my mother. If I achieved something good then I was ungrateful, rubbing her face in the opportunities she made for me. If I failed then it was a direct reflection on how she'd done as a mother. Furthermore, she had raised me to be independent, but still expected me to be her subordinate. It was confusing to maneuver through the paradox of my life.

My leaving to attend college challenged everything my mother felt. I was growing beyond her and though that was what she'd expected me to do, she didn't want to let go. Her controlling nature battled a raging storm inside of her. The anger she was displaying because of my dorm assignment was a manifestation of her inner fight.

Looking around the room my mother proclaimed, "All this is mine. You won't be taking a fucking thing with you, except your slutty clothes."

I didn't know what to say. I was worried that if I spoke, the joy would be too apparent in my voice, pissing her off worse. Still, I hadn't expected to bring anything with me. Goodness knows I didn't want anything from her. She already felt she was entitled to something for simply giving birth to me; I didn't need to give her more reason to consider me indebted to her.

Of course, I had intended to take my clothes, especially since I bought most of my wardrobe. I began working when I was fifteen years old and since then, I was tasked with buying anything personal that I wanted, including clothes. None of my outfits were slutty either, but my mother was just trying to ruffle my feathers. My mother would never allow me to purchase something without her consent and everything I wore had received her seal of approval.

"I know you think you're an adult now, but you're not," my mother was extremely agitated. "You won't be able to do whatever you want, whenever you want to either. There are going to be rules and people to enforce those rules," she threatened.

"I know," I said softly.

"You know, you know," she mocked. "You think you're so smart. You know *everything*, don't you?"

She came rushing towards me, but stopped abruptly, just short of ramming me in the face with her own. Her breath was hot on my skin and reeked of alcohol. Alcohol! My mother was never really one to drink because she didn't like to lose control, so this was new. When had she begun to drink and how much? Something clicked inside my head and I understood she was using booze to cope with her stress.

"If you do anything wrong then they'll kick you out and where do you think you'll go then? Huh? Huh?" My mother's eyes were blood shot and glossy; her movements were erratic and as unpredictable as her mood. She turned away from me and gestured grandly to my room. "I promise you, it won't be back here; no, ma'am, not here."

I just looked at her. I tried to keep my face blank of all expression and, honestly, I was too afraid to speak, so I kept silent. I hoped she would run out of steam soon and leave me to my homework, but I had no faith in that outcome. I wasn't that lucky on her best day, so I was more certain of sucky odds with her intoxicated.

"You want to be grown and you want to be in charge," she accused me angrily, "Then you get to be. You won't get any help from us. You hear me?"

"Yes, mother," I responded gingerly.

I knew that my mother wouldn't contribute to the education and college expenses I expected. Thankfully, I didn't even have to file for financial aid. If I had, then my mother would have used that to control me since it would have been linked to her release of tax information. Perhaps that was why my grandma had done what she did?

When my grandma died, she'd denied my mother any inheritance in order to ensure my future. She took the legal steps to have all of her possessions and assets liquidated, placing all the funds into a college fund for me. Since my grandparents had been well-off, it was more than enough to cover my tuition, supplies, and cost-of-living for the entire period I expected to be a student. Upon graduating, the balance of the fund would be paid out directly to me in order to assist me with starting my adult life.

My grandmother had stipulated that I needed to earn a degree, any degree – Associate's, Bachelor's, or Master's – before the money could be paid out to me. She'd also made certain that none of the money would ever go to my mom. In the event that something happened to me, the fund would be given out as grant and scholarship money to other students. This did *not* sit well with my mother.

"You're on your own. Do you understand?" she questioned me intensely.

"Yes," I said in almost a whisper.

"Good, because the day you turn eighteen, I want you gone," she instructed.

"What?" I managed in a tiny voice, feeling stunned.

My mouth dropped open; I hadn't expected that. I had expected to live at home until I could move into my dorms. I would graduate high school in the end of May, but I wasn't able to move into my dorm until August. My mind start to scramble with what my options might be; did I even have any options? If grandma was still alive then I could have stayed with her, but now, who could I turn to? Maybe I could stay at Angie's or Cedric's?

My mother started to laugh. She was quite aware of the impact her words had had on me and I'd given her the exact reaction she expected. "That's right. You get what you want, you ungrateful wretch. You wanted to be independent so I'm giving it to you. I want you out of my house next Thursday; happy birthday, Tiffany!"

My mother cackled and hooted as she finally left my room. She was hollering profanities and threats even as she moved down the hall towards her own room. I was glad she had left me alone, but I was in no state of mind to focus on my schooling now. I had too much to figure out. I had to make arrangements for a new place to live and I only had a week to do it.

I had so many questions with unknown answers. For one, would I have any money? I had a stock pile in my mother's room from working, but the question remained, would she give it to me? If she didn't, what would I do? Perhaps I needed to come up with a plan to try to nab some of it. Thankfully, I still had some hidden cash in my little stash. I hadn't used very much of it when I bought that ill-fated camera, but was it enough?

Though I was fretful and worried about what was to come, I had to take a moment to find my silver lining. It was there; she was letting me go. She was pissy and mean, but she was allowing me to leave without the fight I had expected. I'd live on the streets until my dorm was ready if I had to; I didn't care. I'd take the streets if it meant she was letting go and it sure seemed like she was.

However, as the days passed, it became more evident that my mother didn't really intend to let me go. It seemed more like she was using the idea of my liberation as a carrot she was dangling in front of me, trying to tantalize me into some craziness that she had imagined. I didn't understand what she was trying to accomplish or what exactly she wanted from me, but I knew instinctively that it wasn't good.

The tension was high and growing higher with each day. I struggled to maintain some sense of perspective in order to control my own emotions while staying focused on my responsibilities. This was supposed to be such a momentous time of life for me, celebrating my birthday, graduation, and going to college, but there wasn't anything magical about it. The heavy guilt my mother laid on me sucked all joy from my heart.

Nothing about me or my life was ever good enough for my mom and this was no exception. As the week passed, even the slightest of nuances took on significant meaning to my mother and managed to cause issues. If I appeared to be sad, then my mother said I was trying to make her feel guilty for giving me what I wanted; my freedom. If I appeared to be happy then she attributed it to my pleasure in hurting her since clearly she was the only one upset about my leaving her. Even saying I loved her didn't help.

She'd usually start our ill-fated conversations by telling me, "I love you."

"I love you, too," I'd tell her honestly, unsuspecting. I don't know why I didn't catch on quicker; maybe I just wanted to believe her.

"Not as much as I love you," she'd tell me morosely.

"Mom, stop," I'd say. "You know I love you very much."

"Maybe, but you'll *never* love me as much as I love you," she'd say. "One day you're going to leave me and I'd *never* leave you."

"I'm not leaving you, mom. I'm just going to college," I'd reply. I was careful not to mention that I was leaving sooner, even before I graduated high school because of her choice, not mine. "I'll call and write all the time plus we'll visit each other."

"No you won't," she'd continue. "You're going to forget all about me. You don't *really* love me; not like I love you. I would *never* forget you or leave you, so that proves I love you more."

Ugh! It was so frustrating, especially because I couldn't win and she knew it too. Nothing I could say or do would make this situation any better; only worse. Each encounter was emotionally, mentally, and even physically taxing for me.

"I could always go with you," she'd suggest.

"Mom, you have to let me grow up some time," I'd try to say.

"See, you *don't* love me."

I just felt defeated. I'd close my eyes in exasperation, but I knew I had to keep myself locked up tight. If I made one small error then she'd pounce. She was egging me on to react and any reaction I had would be a terrible blunder. I sighed heavily and just endured in silence. This new game of hers was cruel and I almost wished she'd just hit me instead.

If she hit me then the pain would be temporary; definitive and swift. This new emotional abuse was horrible. It was like a plague and it lingered even after the episode. I was used to her playing games, but she'd definitely amped it up to a new level. This uncharted territory made me feel very unsafe and unstable. It made me feel sick and I knew it was a matter of time before I fell hard on my face.

***

I was sitting in the waiting room with my mother's eagle eye on me. Things had been different between us lately. I couldn't explain how; I just felt it and it made my skin crawl. I didn't know how I was going to explain it to Dr. Maxwell or why I'd even consider telling him. There was nothing he could do. No matter how many times I solicited his aid in my situation, he was unable to comply.

When the receptionist told me that he was ready and I could go back into the doctor's office, my mother looked at me as though she wanted to say something. She glanced at the receptionist briefly then back to me. She sighed deeply, as though resigned, and relaxed back into her chair with the magazine she was flipping through. I blinked in confusion then turned to meet with Dr. Maxwell.

When I entered his room, I took my usual seat. We had long since dispensed with formalities, so we simply asked after each other. We checked in with one another and asked about what had happened since we last saw one another. Eventually, we worked our way into the nitty-gritty and tackled the business for which I had come.

"Sometimes when I'm standing there with my mother screaming so close to my face that her spit showers me, it's like. . . " I struggled to put it into words.

"It's like what?" the doctor encouraged me.

"It's like I'm trapped inside a movie and I want to hit rewind to start the scene again. I feel like my body is rapidly twisting back and forth, like someone possessed, though no part of me is actually moving. I can hear my own scream as it echoes through my mind though I don't make a sound. It's like I'm somewhere inside myself, watching; unable to take control of things happening around me."

"Like an out-of-body experience," he probed.

"Maybe," I sighed and looked out the window. "I don't know. I don't think so."

I watched the birds chirping and hopping on a branch outside the office window. I knew these birds well; grackles. Despite my dislike for them, they made me wonder what it would be like to be a bird. Would life be simpler than as a human? Surely, there are trials and tribulations connected with the constant hunt for food and threat from predators, but what would that feel like? At any time a bird could just stretch its wings and take flight. I'd like to do that. I'd like to spread my wings and take flight.

"Tiffany," Dr. Maxwell called my name to refocus my attention.

"Sorry," I said, chagrined. He just smiled and leaned back in his chair. "It's not like I'm outside of my body, looking down on the scene while it plays out. It's more like I'm trapped in a small, dark place somewhere inside my head, looking out through my own eyes from a distance."

"Interesting," he commented.

"Not really," I told him. "It makes me feel insignificant."

"Do you think you're insignificant?" I hated when he did his doctor thing. Ugh.

"No," I replied annoyed. Then I looked at my hands as I fidgeted with my nails and added, "Maybe; sometimes, yeah."

"Everybody -" I cut him off before he could add to that comment.

"Don't tell me it's normal; that *everybody* feels like that at times," I looked at him in warning. "*Nothing* about it feels normal."

Dr. Maxwell took a moment to collect his self and then he said, "You live under extraordinary pressure. Considering your circumstances, you're dealing very well. You're exhibiting signs of anxiety and depression, but what you're experiencing *is* normal for those conditions, I assure you."

"The medication you gave me doesn't seem to help," I told him.

"It isn't meant to stop you from feeling," he reminded me. "I don't want to make you a zombie."

"I know," I countered. "It's meant to take the edge off so I can better manage my feelings."

"Exactly," Dr. Maxwell nodded at me in affirmation.

"It's not helping," I reiterated. I paused a moment then remarked, "Or maybe things are just getting worse."

"What do you mean?" He moved to the edge of his chair in concern. "What's getting worse, Tiffany?"

"Everything. Nothing," I answered. I sighed in exasperation. "Something is *changing*."

"Changing how?" he pushed.

"I don't know. I'm not sure yet, but I can *feel* it. I know that something is coming, but I'm not sure what. I'm not sure how to stop it or how to protect myself from it."

"Does your mother still expect you to move out on Thursday?" he asked me.

"She is still saying that, but I doubt she's going to let me leave when the time comes," I told him. I knew he thought maybe I was overly sensitive about the upcoming change to my life, but that wasn't the case, so I added, "That's not it though. There's something I'm just not getting."

"I don't know what to say," he replied.

"I know and I don't expect you to say or do anything," I said kindly.

"I wish your mother hadn't found that camera," Dr. Maxwell told me. "That would have ended all speculation and given us the legal evidence to charge your mother with her crimes."

"It was my mistake," I acknowledged.

"I'm truly sorry," he said as he reached out and patted my hand. "I feel so useless."

"Yeah, join the club."

"Have you thought of anything else that you might be able to do?" he asked.

"No, but I guess it won't matter in a few days anyway," I said looking around the room. I liked the room because it was welcoming. The doctor had tried to make sure the décor was inviting and comforting; he'd succeeded.

"Yeah, I guess not," he replied sounding sullen. "Where will you be staying?"

I was already on a different train of thought so I ignored his question, saying, "You know, they say you sort of teach people how to treat you."

The doctor's interest was piqued. "Can you elaborate on this for me please?"

"Well, I mean your response to the way people treat you sort of sets the bar for what's expected and what you're personal limitations are, you know?" I began. "Like how much crap you're willing to take from someone before you get angry or what's taboo altogether."

"Hmmm, interesting," Dr. Maxwell said. "I see where you're going with this. You're saying that if someone hit you and you downplay it, saying 'it's okay' then they think it really is okay and are prone to hitting you again, right?"

"Exactly," I confirmed. "Well, the thing I don't really get is how I taught my mother to hit me."

"Oh," Dr. Maxwell said as his face turned red. "I'm sorry. That was an insensitive example on my part."

"No; no, it wasn't," I reassured him. "It was exactly right and appropriate for the situation."

"I certainly wasn't implying that you invited your mother to abuse you," Dr. Maxwell said slightly embarrassed.

"I know," I told him. "It's okay, really."

The doctor looked upset and unconvinced of my approval, but he remained silent and let me continue with my thought.

"Actually, that highlights my thought in a way. I mean, children don't really get a say in how their parents treat them. Often, they don't get a say in how anyone treats them and really no one takes a child seriously; they're easily dismissed."

"Is that how you feel; dismissed?" he asked me.

I decided not to answer his direct question, but to continue with my thought instead. "By the time a child is old enough to have an opinion about their behavior, the patterns are already in place. The expectations of the child and the parameters of his or her relationships are already firmly formed. All this happens before the child gets to be considered an active participant in their own life."

"I agree with that to a point," the doctor told me. "Regardless of our pasts, at some point we all have to take responsibility for our own actions. We cannot control what others do or don't do, but we have control of ourselves."

"I hear you and yes, I agree," I told him, "but tell me this, should I be held responsible for my behavior when I've essentially been rendered powerless? Is it fair to hold me accountable for my actions when they're always being dictated to me?"

Dr. Maxwell looked at me with a pout. I knew he didn't like my spin on things.

I continued by asking, "At what point do you consider me mature enough to take responsibility; it is an age or an action? It is like potty training; if I'm old enough to tell you I have to potty then I'm ready to be trained or is it like voting where I have to be eighteen in order to have that privilege?"

I stopped, looking at his tired face for a few minutes before I added, "Should I be held accountable for maintaining the relationships and behaviors I was groomed to have or do I have the right to restructure all of my relationships? Am I solely responsible for rebuilding new connections, expectations, and limitations?"

"Tiffany, I'm not sure how to answer that, but I guess maybe the better question is whether or not you think you're accountable and why," he replied.

"No, I don't believe I am," I answered. "No one hears me when I speak; they dismiss me. My mother keeps such a tight rein on me that I don't have any room to have my own thoughts or behaviors to be held accountable for."

"But you do have your own thoughts and you are in control of your own behaviors," Dr. Maxwell told me.

"I don't believe that," I countered. "My thoughts don't count. Being a minor means I'm a child and my mother is the adult, and therefore, always more reliable. My behavior is controlled by the fear I live with. I only do as I'm told because if I don't, she'll beat me and no one will stop her."

I looked Dr. Maxwell directly in the eyes and asked, "What could I possibly have done in my life that taught my mother to beat me? How can I be accountable for my actions when I'm not even considered a person? How will that all change come Thursday when I turn eighteen and have to take charge of my life? Am I going to be held accountable when I've been taught how to problem solve or make proper decisions?"

We sat quietly for a while. Then the doctor said, "Do you feel like I'm helping at all? Do you feel like you're getting anything out of therapy?"

"Sometimes," I said honestly. "Sometimes it's just helpful to have someone listen and care about how I feel."

"Thanks," he answered quietly.

I smiled at him then looked away, "Sometimes, it's just nice to get away from her and be safely locked in here, where she can't get to me for an hour or so."

Dr. Maxwell seemed less happy with that remark, but he seemed resolved to accept it for what it was; the truth. I couldn't help feeling sad. I knew Dr. Maxwell had good intentions and I knew he'd do more if he could, but it didn't matter. This was the reality of my situation and this was how it would stay. I had to learn to live with it and so did he.

CHAPTER FIFTEEN

It was the day before my eighteenth birthday. My mother still said she expected to move out the next day, so I'd begun to handle my last minute preparations. I had worked it out with Angie's parents and I'd be staying with them until I could move into my dorm. They'd be expecting me after school.

I wasn't sure what had caused the tension in my house to escalate, but it had. Though my mother stuck to her guns, saying she wanted me to get out, she was pissed that I was trying to leave. She was offended that I was actually doing what she told me to do, though I wasn't really sure why. Perhaps she just couldn't accept losing control of the situation and seeing her dictatorship come to an end. At any rate, she stuck to me like flies on shit; watching everything I did with intense scrutiny.

As evening drew on and the closer we got to my departure, the more tense things became. My anxiety seemed directly proportionate to the tension levels, as did my mother's anger. The longer I worked to get everything together and the more she crowded me while I did it, the more hostile the situation became. Ultimately, my mother exploded, causing a heated argument and physical altercation.

I don't really know what transpired, since I felt sort of disconnected. I just remember hearing myself talk back to my mother despite my inner voice telling me to shut up. When my mother started to throw punches, I actually did a good job of deflecting them, but not good enough; probably because I was sort of blacking out, mentally detached from the whole situation. It wasn't long before my mother had me pinned to the ground.

She sat straddled on top of me, using her weight to try to hold me down. She had a butcher's knife poised over me though I couldn't recall when she'd grabbed it. We were struggling over it, both of us trying to gain possession of the knife. As we fought, I knew this was the final play in our game. The moment of retribution had finally arrived.

"Get off me!" I screamed.

"Make me, you little bitch," she bellowed back.

I was bucking wildly in an attempt to break her hold. The knife bobbed dangerously close to my face more times than I wanted to say, but it didn't stop me from trying to toss her off my body. If anything, it made me more panicked and I worked harder to buck her off. I knew without a doubt that if I stopped fighting I was surely dead, so I was going to give her all I had.

"Why do you hate me so much?" I questioned, as the knife sliced a small nick into my collarbone. Somehow, I managed to keep my composure and force her hands away from me before she could cause additional damage. "What could I possibly have done that you'd want to kill me?"

"You exist; that's enough," she glared at me icily.

Seeing the loathing in her eyes, I felt like she gave me a physical blow. I flinched away which only made her laugh. Her laughter caused her to relax, giving me a moment to drop my guard against her attack. I weakened my grasp on her, uncertain how long I'd have before she resumed her strike. In that brief moment, I tried to reassess the situation.

I didn't want to hurt my mother. I loved her no matter what she'd said or done; no matter what I'd said or done. Her words hurt me deeply because of this love. My anger was subsiding and I blinked my eyes quickly to try to clear the tears that threatened to fall. I was still in perilous danger; this was no time to lose focus.

"I'm that horrible?" I asked sadly. I almost choked on the words.

My mother stopped laughing. She looked directly in my eyes and said clearly, "Yes."

It was enough. I saw the truth in her eyes and I knew that she meant it. My heart broke irreversibly, completely. She couldn't have done more damage to me than she had with that simple confession. Even if my mother had stabbed the cold knife directly into my heart, she couldn't have cut me worse. I was shattered.

My mind spun, but now I had to decide what to do; what did it meant to me, knowing she hated me? Instinctively I knew that one of us was not going to walk away from this fight. This was the moment we'd been working up to my entire life. This would be the moment that defined us as people and decided our fates.

"I love you, mom," I said weakly, dropping my hands away from her. I felt tired; tired to the very depth of my soul. I was tired of the games and the constant fighting; tired of living, if that was what you could call this existence.

"You shut up!" my mother screamed then she back-handed me across the face. I knew that my mother thought this was a great insult; a degrading gesture of sorts. It was done to make me feel subservient to her; literally giving her the upper hand.

I simply accepted the assault. The burn to my face was nothing compared to the pain in my heart. "I'm not going to fight you anymore."

I didn't feel like I was giving up. It felt more like I was giving in. Though I said nothing defining or notable, I'd decided what I wanted; what my fate would be. I was resolved and simply accepted my choice. In doing so, I no longer had the urge to resist.

"You're stupid," her voice was full of disgust. "You're weak and pathetic."

"Maybe," I answered, "but I'm not a killer." My mother looked at me in surprise; bewildered. "I love you and I refuse to be the one to take your life."

"So who's to stop me from taking yours?" she said with a sick smile.

"No one," I replied. "I give you my life willingly."

"Like I said, *stupid*," she repeated. I wasn't able to discern my mother's emotional state of mind. I guess it really didn't matter to me anymore. I'd never be able to force, earn, or gain my mother's love and I was tired of trying.

"No matter what you do, I'm not going to fight you anymore," I told her calmly and I knew I meant it. I knew who I was. I knew how I wanted to live my life and now, I knew how I wanted to die.

My mother just made a *humph* noise at me. "You'd let me kill you?"

"I'd rather give you my life than give you my soul."

"So be it," she said, lifting the knife above her. Without hesitation or restraint she plunged it towards me.

I felt the knife as it embedded into my shoulder, but before it cut too deeply, it was torn to the side. I screamed in agony as light and dark cast shadows across my sight. My world started to glaze over and the motion of the world was a blur. I felt detached and the pain burned white hot, stunning me and preventing my ability to think. Squeezing my eyes shut tight, I struggled to control my breathing and endure the pain coursing through me. I could feel myself slipping over the edge as darkness enveloped me, taking me to a place of unconsciousness.

When I came to, the first thing I noticed was the goo caking my hands; making my fingers stick together. I soon realized that the goo was blood and that it was all around me. I looked at the blood in confusion and it dawned on me that the spill seemed to be getting larger. As I paid close attention to the growing pool of blood, I wondered where it was coming from; whose blood was all over the floor? Was it my blood?

I was fascinated and even a little excited. I wanted to see just how big the pool could get. How much blood was actually in a human body? I'd heard somewhere that it was enough to fill one to two one-gallon milk jugs. Gross, I thought as I envisioned pure white milk swirled with streaks of deep red blood. A wave of nausea struck me and I closed my eyes to regroup.

When I opened my eyes again, I felt a little more attentive. I noticed there was something next to me, on the other edge of the blood pool. I wasn't certain, but I thought it was my mother. Yes, it was. I saw my mother lying still, staring at me with her lifeless eyes; a knife protruding from her chest. Someone had stabbed her several times in a small cluster around her heart. I knew instantly that the wounds had caused her death. She was the source of the blood.

The blood entranced me. I watched it as it flowed from underneath my mother and I thought of a rushing river. I wondered if blood behaved the same way as water. I wondered if it ebbed and flowed in the same manner. It must. I mean, a person's blood can become thicker because of a lack of water intake or because of an ailment like cholesterol, so it'd be feasible to have both fast and slow flowing blood due to its consistency; just like a river.

Nawh, not like a river; more like a hot springs, I corrected myself. It'd be more like a hot springs because the blood was hot, especially next to the cold floor. I was intrigued by the warmth the blood emitted and how you could feel the difference in temperature compared to its surrounding. It wasn't like the blood was steaming or anything; just that I noticed the difference; interesting.

I slowly worked my way over to my mother. I tried to remember what had happened, but the memories hurt too much and I shied away from them. The sting was too much to bear as I thought of how she'd looked at me and readily stabbed me. I began to sob inconsolably; not that anyone was there to comfort me. As I sat overlooking my dead mother, I reached for the knife and withdrew it from her chest.

The pain I felt was overwhelming. Though my mother had been the cause of all my suffering, I said, "I'm sorry, mom."

I wasn't really sure what I was sorry for. I was numb, but the sorrow that gripped me was heavy; like a physical weight. I sobbed, wishing things were different. Despite all her failings and short comings, I mourned the loss of my mother. I also mourned the mother I had never had, but whom I had wanted none the less. The need I had for my mother to be a part of my life just seemed to be getting larger and larger.

I wasn't really aware of time. I had no way of knowing just how long I'd sat there, weeping over my mother's corpse. I felt so tired and I was growing colder. Eventually, I curled up next to my mom, resting my head against her. I wrapped her dead arm around me as best I could, but it was just like it always was; lifeless and uncooperative. I finally just accepted things and let her arm fall away from me, crying harder.

It seemed like an eternity had passed when I felt someone tapping my shoulder. I could hear someone calling in the distance, but it was so far away; I couldn't seem to make out what they were saying. I worked hard to pull myself together enough to look up in search of the caller and to stop the irritating tapping. When I did, I looked into the distraught face of my step-dad and noticed a blur of blue as it moved into the room behind him.

***

I found myself in the mental ward once again, only this time it wasn't at the hospital. It was still undecided as to which facility I'd call my final home, but for now, I was here, in the Breckenridge Institute for the Criminally Insane. I'd be here until the conclusion of my trial. Not that it was much of a trial. They had decided I was insane, so really it was more about trying to decide what to do with me.

It was a different experience in this mental facility than it had been at the hospital. Things were obviously more rigid and structured, but they were also lonelier. In the hospital, you were encouraged to partake in activities and socialize. Here, you spent most of the time in your assigned room, hidden away behind the bolted metal door and barred windows.

As you can imagine, most of my time was spent in isolation. Outside of the staff or legal aid, no visitors came to see me. This only compounded my loneliness, but it was what I'd expected. I'd been a prisoner my entire life and isolation made things easier for me, albeit lonelier. No one came to see me at my house, so I knew no one would visit me here either.

I was never in league with the prom queen and I was far from popular. People seemed to know who I was because there were always rumors and gossip flying around. What my peers didn't get from events at school, they'd get from their parents. My mother usually originated the stories that were passed around. She kept a healthy flow of tales that went from her to the community, to parents, and then to the kids.

By my estimation, most people were surprised to hear the news about me. Most were like, "she seems so quiet and well-mannered, but I guess it's the one you least suspect that are the worst." No matter how I behaved, the rumors were always treated as gospel and, therefore, stuck. Though Angie and Cedric ignored the tales as they either suspected, or chose to ignore, the truth, most others didn't. I'm sure I was right where everyone expected me to end up.

When I finally did receive a visitor, I wasn't surprised to see it was Dr. Maxwell. I think I was more surprised that he hadn't come sooner. Of course, one look at him clued me in as to the probable cause for his delay. He looked miserable and I felt bad for him. I guessed he blamed himself for my circumstances, but I knew it wasn't his fault.

Though Dr. Maxwell had been in denial, I had not. I knew that this was one of the inevitable outcomes of my explosive relationship with my mother. I thought he had understood that too, but obviously, that hadn't been the case. I always knew that man was more optimistic than he should have been.

The trouble was that Dr. Maxwell believed in the system. He was a part of the system so of course he had to believe in it. If he didn't then what did that say about his chosen profession or life's work? Actually, his optimism was one of the things I liked about him. I admired his unending hope and his continued faith.

"Well howdy, stranger," I addressed him pleasantly. "Boy, you've aged." I tried to get him to smile, but he was not interested in friendly banter.

"Tiffany," he said forlornly. "Tiffany, I -"

I held my hand up, gesturing for him to stop. "There's nothing you could've done to prevent this."

Dr. Maxwell looked like he was in physical pain from my words. "I just -". He gave up before he began. He cast his gaze to the ground looking forlorn and tired.

"I told you before, the only ending to all this was the death of one or both us."

"I didn't really believe that," Dr. Maxwell said in dismay. He looked at me with pleading eyes.

"I know," I smiled encouragingly at him, "but I guess I just have to decide now whether I'm glad it was her or if it should've been me who died." I sighed deeply.

Dr. Maxwell looked down again. He looked haggard and drained. This whole thing had obviously been harder on him than it had been on me; I wasn't kidding when I'd said he looked older than he had before. I think he'd come in order to try to console me and instead, I found I was consoling him. Strangely, trying to help Dr. Maxwell actually did help me somehow. I felt more at peace with what had happened and where I had ended up. It all seemed like it was meant to be.

"You have to let this go," I told him when he looked at me again. His eyes were glossy and I could tell he was fighting tears. "You did everything you could and it was enough. It was enough for me and I'm okay."

The doctor gave me a look of disbelief. Though I was telling him the truth, he remained unconvinced. I knew his inability to believe me was because he felt responsible. His guilt was eating him alive.

"You need to forgive yourself for whatever fault you think you have. This is where I knew I'd eventually end up," I admitted and then after a small pause I added, "If I didn't die first."

"I won't be continuing your care, Tiffany," the doctor told me quietly. I nodded at him thoughtfully; I had expected as much, especially when a new guy working in the insane asylum came to speak with me. Dr. Maxwell's extended absence just solidified my belief, so I didn't really need this verbal confirmation. "And, I won't be coming back to see you again."

"Yeah, I figured that," I smiled humorlessly. I rested my hand on his upper arm and squeezed it reassuringly. "Thanks for everything, but I'm okay. It's okay."

"I wish I could have," he fought to say all the things he felt. His struggle was difficult to watch and I wanted to make it easier for him, but I knew it was a battle he'd have to fight alone. These were his demons taunting him, not mine.

"I know," I told him. "There's nothing you have to say. Really," I smiled at him kindly, "go in pace, Dr. Maxwell and enjoy your life."

He started to turn towards the doorway, but then stopped. After a slight hesitation, he turned and hugged me tightly. After a long moment, he released me then abruptly left my room. I stood alone in his wake, as the silence replacing his presence engulfed me. I'd miss Dr. Maxwell and I truly wished him well. I'd pray for him to find his peace; he deserved that.

I deserved it and I actually found peace in the silence. I really couldn't complain as no one was beating me and just as I had always wished for, people mostly left me alone. I spent a lot of time sleeping, especially since the medications they gave me were so sedating. I also spent a lot of time just aimlessly staring out the barred window. I liked to watch the birds in flight, the squirrels at play, and the trees as they danced in the wind.

I missed the feel of the breeze on my face, but I soaked up the sunshine that poured in. I liked how it felt to just close my eyes and let the warmth wash over me. It felt healing and cleansing. The silence felt like a blanket that swaddled me from the craziness of the world. In my little room, I really was okay.

CHAPTER SIXTEEN

As I walked into the open room, watched intently by guards, I saw my step-father through the glass window. He was on the other side of the wall that separated prisoners from visitors. Some jailhouses allowed inmates to receive guests in a common area, but this wasn't a normal jailhouse; it was a nut house. Therefore, precautions were taken here to ensure the safety of everyone involved.

These precautions dictated that the moderately-sized room be partitioned off through the middle of the space. Essentially, the partitioned wall consisted of a solid divider with bullet-proof glass on the top portion and a solid enclosure on the bottom. A long table lined both sides of the wall where the glass half met the solid section. The tables were then subdivided into sections to offer a bit of privacy to each of the prisoners while they met with their visitors.

The subdivisions were meant to give each inmate and their guests their own space, while still allowing the guards to see everything that transpired. The prisoner would talk to their visitor over telephones that worked as intercoms. The phone cords were very short and could be retracted with the push of a button if the guards had any concerns.

The room had guards on both sides of the partitioning wall. This was meant to provide supervision to the inmates and further protection to the guests. The room was designed to allow multiple exchanges to occur at once while still limiting the number of visits for easier control. The only other additions to the room were chairs that were bolted to the floor.

Nothing was left to chance. There wasn't anything available for someone to hurt themselves or anyone else with. In addition to these precautions, other guards monitored the room from behind a two-way mirror along the back wall. This was only on the side of those incarcerated at the asylum.

I couldn't help wondering about this whole setup. I wondered how much was really monitored and if we might even be on video. Did they monitor or record the conversations being held and, if so, were the exchanges valid in a court of law? That was something to look into, I thought to myself curiously.

I sat in one of the partial cubicles as my step-dad gestured for me to pick up the phone. Lifting the phone to my ear, I felt numb. I truly had no sentiment for this man; nothing. I was neither angry nor happy. In fact, if I were to categorize what I felt then it would best be described as confused. I saw no reason for my step-dad to be here and I wasn't sure if I really wanted to speak with him.

At first, we sat there quietly, just staring at one another. It felt awkward, to say the least. I hadn't seen him since my sentencing which I was okay with. I honestly never expected to see him again. With my mother gone, there was no longer any reason for us to interact. There was nothing binding us to each other. I was finally nothing to him, just like he'd always wanted.

"How are you?" he asked, looking uncomfortable.

I looked at him for a moment longer. Was he really trying to make small talk; here, now? This all seemed a bit absurd to me, to be honest. There was no love lost between us and no reason for us to continue communicating. I fought the urge to just get up and walk away.

"I'm okay," I said in a tired voice.

"You look exhausted," he pointed out the obvious. I just nodded slightly and sort of looked around. I was unsure what he was trying to circle around to, but I could see there was something he wanted to say. I wished I knew how to make him get to his point so I could end this awkward, not to mention unwanted, discussion.

I sighed heavily. Turning my attention back to my step-dad, I decided to cut to the chase. I looked at him expectantly and asked directly, "Why are you here?"

"I wanted to see how you were doing," he said anxiously. "They're treating you good?"

"Good enough," I replied noncommittally. "Is that it then?"

My step-father cleared his throat nervously, looking around to see if our conversation had an audience. Then he looked me in the eye, bowed his head slightly and said, "I came to say I'm sorry."

"For what?" I asked, with a spark of anger. "Enabling my mother to abuse me, or supporting her when she lied about it?"

"Yeah, for that," he swallowed hard. I noticed the sweat beading up on his forehead.

My step-dad started to fidget with his hands. Though he'd never seemed bothered in the past by a conscience, he seemed to have developed one since we had last met. I was sort of fascinated which lessened my ager, though my instincts were all screaming at me to beware. This was a man not to be trusted.

"Why now?" I asked suspiciously. "Why, after all this time and craziness, are you sorry now?"

"Well," he started. His voice was scratchy and he had to clear his throat again. "I feel like I could've done something to help you."

"There were a lot of things you could've done to help me," I reminded him coldly.

"I guess," he said in a small voice as he looked down.

"You *know*," I said pointedly. I didn't want to torture him, but I was determined to hold him accountable, at least to me.

"I don't want to fight. I want to tell you I'm sorry, but specifically I'm sorry for letting you go to jail," he swallowed hard. He dabbed the sweat beading up on his forehead and the action just made him all the more loathsome to me.

"What do you mean?" I asked cautiously. "What do you mean you're 'sorry for *letting* me go to jail'?"

"I mean, I'm sorry you're here," he was fidgeting in his chair now. He was hesitant and his anxiety had grown, but he finally managed to add, "and I'm not."

"Why should you be here?" I looked at him directly. This was why he'd come. I felt it in my very bones.

"Because I was the one who killed her," he said, unable to meet my eyes.

I was stunned into silence, unsure if I had heard him correctly. Then he said it again and it was like he couldn't stop. That confession was like the cork being blown off his tightly-bound horde of secrets; everything just bubbled forth after he finally admitted this truth. I sat befuddled, focusing hard to understand the words my step-dad continued to say.

My step-dad continued with his confession by telling me that my mother had hated me because I was the constant reminder of what she'd lost. Apparently, she'd been madly in love with my biological father; so much so that she ended her promiscuous ways. As they'd begun to plan a future together, my mother felt like she was receiving everything she'd wanted out of life. That was when she got pregnant and he tossed her aside.

My father disgraced my mother and refused to acknowledge me as his own. He told everyone that my mother was a whore and that he'd caught her in bed with another man. My mother had vehemently denied the allegations, but the damage was done. Her previous reputation had been confirmation enough to make his lies their reality. No one would listen to my mother's side of the story.

My father played the victim like a champ, I was told, and everyone turned on my mother. My father played the martyr, saying he just couldn't believe my mother would stoop so low that she'd knowingly trap him into marrying her while she was pregnant with another man's child. When she swore her love and loyalty, offering to have a paternity test done, my father had dismissed her. He had acted outraged by the idea of taking a paternity test, saying he had nothing to prove; he knew the truth.

My mother was devastated. She contemplated getting an abortion, thinking this would make my father want her again, but my grandmother wouldn't hear of it. My step-dad told me that my grandmother had forced my mom to keep me, which added to her animosity towards me. By forcing her to keep me, my mother was convinced I'd destroyed her one chance at true love though even my step-dad admitted her resentment was unjustified. He confessed that both he and my mom knew it didn't matter; my father would have left eventually, no matter what.

My step-dad explained that my mom had struggled for years. She wanted to be a good mother and to get past the negative feelings she had for me, but she couldn't get past the pain she felt whenever she looked at me. I was a physical representation of the abandonment that consumed her. I was the constant reminder of all she had lost.

When my father cast her aside, everyone followed suit. She hadn't just lost the love of her life, but her place in her social group and all the friends she thought she'd had. No one wanted to be stuck with her and her baby when they could be out partying. They were young and they wanted to enjoy it. To add insult to injury, it'd only been a few days before my father started seeing my mother's best friend. My step-dad said that was how they knew it wasn't really about me; they'd been sneaking around with each other behind her back for some time.

Since my mother was a single parent, she lived with my grandmother. My step-dad said he believed that was what had helped to curb my mother's abusive tendencies while I was little. He said my grandmother was always very involved with me and tried very hard to help take the stress of parenting off my mom. Even when he came into the picture, my grandmother continued to help support them and to provide free childcare for me. When my grandmother died, the little bit of grounding my mother seemed to have had died with her.

My step-dad had loved my mother with his entire being, vowing to do whatever it took to make her happy. When my mother found and married my step-dad, he knew she didn't love him. Much to his chagrin, she'd always been brutally honest about her feelings regarding him. He knew full well that she didn't love him and never expected to, but he loved her enough to dedicate his life to trying to change her heart.

My mom had been grateful to my step-dad for not only accepting her in her loveless state, but for accepting me as well. Her abandonment issues made my step-dad's devotion intoxicating and that need is what ultimately won my mother's hand in marriage. My step-dad didn't care that my mom assumed he was her last chance to have her own family because it meant she'd give herself to him. That was all he wanted.

My mother was happy for a time. My step-dad gave her the family she'd wanted and made it possible for her to leave my grandmother's home. Of course, this eventually wasn't enough and over time, my mother grew more resentful. This resentment led to her anger and then unleashed her hostility.

My mother was in a marriage of convenience, not love. She was forced to care for a child she never wanted. This all took a toll on her and her relationships with my grandmother, step-dad, and me. The more out-of-control she felt, the more she tried to dominate. Losing my grandmother only added to my mother's stress and exacerbated her situation, increasing her need for control. Most people interpreted her actions as grief over my grandmother's passing, so her descent into abuse was not obvious to anyone.

At first, my step-dad didn't really think much of my mother's growing hostility. He thought she was being a strict parent and couldn't see the abuse for what it really was. He had no means by which to measure her actions either, so he just accepted it. I wasn't his biological child and my mom was female, so he assumed she knew best.

Eventually, he saw it as a potential way for him to win my mother's affections. She always seemed to be more intimate with him when he backed her up. Her sexual availability to him when he supported her unconditionally was a reward he couldn't ignore. My mother's happiness and affection was like a drug to my step-dad. He craved her love desperately, so he was willing to pay any price to receive it.

As time went on, my step-dad grew more aware of the true situation. The increased violence as I matured concerned him, but by then the destructive patterns were in place; he had no idea how to change the situation. He realized the older I got, the more I threatened my mother. I was a younger, prettier version of her; a reminder that she was aging. He said it was just another thorn in her side and one he didn't know how to combat.

Of course, my step-dad neglected to add that he was too weak to stop her. Even if he'd wanted to tell someone and get help to change the situation, he wouldn't betray my mother like that. He was too co-dependent to do anything that might

take her from him. Though he didn't add that into his testimony, we both knew it was true and I read it easily in his
guilty expression.

My step-dad was conflicted and confused; all the while
growing more disheartened. My mother's behavior disgusted
him, but his own compliance was demoralizing. He was
ashamed and embarrassed, but not enough to turn away
from my mom. He was like a moth and she was the flame
that was brighter than any reason or emotion.

When my step-dad found my mother pinning me down with
the knife above me, everything came to a head and he could
no longer ignore the situation. He said he knew he'd never be
able to look at himself in the mirror again if he allowed her to
murder me. He knew I was a good person and he wanted to be
a good person too. The night he killed my mother was his first
and last attempt to save me from the monster she'd become.

My step-dad had entered the room where my mother had
me pinned and watched us struggle over the knife. At first,
he thought this was one of our normal tiffs, but after hearing
the interaction between us, he knew without a doubt that my
mother intended to kill me. The realization made him move
before he could think it through. He raced forward, ramming
her from the side, hoping to knock her away from me before
she could actually stab me. Unfortunately, he was a little too
late.

He hadn't managed to prevent the knife from penetrating,
but he had intervened quickly enough to stop it from entering
too deeply, saving my life. The momentum caused by him
tackling my mom not only cast her off me, but redirected the
knife. The tearing sensation I'd experienced that night was
caused by the knife as it was being yanked to the side, caught
in my mother's movement. The pain that seared through me
had caused me to pass out.

While I'd been unconscious, my mother and step-dad had engaged in battle. My mother scrambled to get the knife in her hand, but my step-dad easily dominated her, taking control of the weapon. Since he was so much larger and stronger than my mom, she really never stood a chance. My mother was enraged and turned all her hatred from me towards him. This show of aggression and hatred was more than my step-dad could handle.

He said he'd been overcome by emotion and in his fit of rage, he plunged the knife directly into my mother's heart. It had felt so good to have a release from the emotions that tormented him that he didn't stop with the first strike. He continued to puncture the knife through her chest over and over again. He said it was like he had no control over his own actions; he'd been on auto-pilot.

When he realized my mother wouldn't hesitate to kill him and then most likely finish the job of killing me, his course of action had been irreversible. It was in that moment that he faced his worst fear and saw himself clearly for the first time. He knew without a doubt that my mother had never loved him, and never would. He'd been her fool and admitting the truth to himself drove him out of his wits. He'd directed all his hurt, rejection, and embarrassment into his assault on her. He kept stabbing her until his anger had evaporated into sorrow.

He had sat there weeping over her body for a few minutes before regaining his composure. Once he realized what he'd done, it was too late; she was gone. He contemplated killing himself, but he heard the sirens; someone had called the police. The sound pulled him from his misery and threw him into intense fear. As he started to look around and take in the scene, he panicked.

He proceeded to tell me how he had raced to the window, looking for the emergency lights. He didn't see anything so he ran to the other room to look out of the windows there. While he was gone, I'd revived and crawled over to my mother's body. When he came back in by me, I had pulled the knife out and was staring at it absently.

At first, my step-dad said he tried to talk to me. He wanted to coax me into getting up and going with him, leaving my mother for the police, but I hadn't been responsive. By the time he was able to get my attention, it was too late. He knew we'd never get away without being seen; our window of escape had passed.

My step-dad had been so frightened by his actions and so panicked at the prospect of being caught that he'd blamed me. He knew everyone would believe him given my history with my mother and my questionable mental health. He explained to the cops that he'd been in the other room with the television on, but he came when he heard screaming. He told them he'd only witnessed the last time I plunged the knife into my mom's chest.

He had a sick, slightly excited smirk on his face as he relayed his interactions with the police. He said he was surprised at how easy it was to deceive them; no one suspected anything different from his account of events. He'd told them he was covered in blood because he'd tried to apply pressure to my mother's heart in order to stop the blood and save her. He said when he realized she was gone, he'd tried to take the knife from me, but I wouldn't comply. My confused state only added validity to his statement.

My step-dad had told them that I attacked my mother, forcing her to try to protect herself. He said he knew this from the yelling we'd done. He said he wasn't sure how I got cut, but he felt it must have happened while my mother was trying to defend herself against me. He said all he really knew was that I had lost my mind and stabbed my mother to death.

I looked at him with my mouth ajar. I was at a loss for words. It was abhorrent enough that he'd witnessed, supported, and allowed my mother to abuse me, but this? Wow. I honestly didn't think he had that kind of ugliness living inside him. I wish he hadn't proven me wrong on that one.

I had never thought much of him. My step-dad was a worthless shell of a man, but this was beyond comprehension. This was reprehensible in ways that were beyond words. I finally saw him as the tiny parasite that he was. Left without my mother to host him, he seemed lost and without purpose.

"I need to know you're okay," he said in a small voice, "and that you forgive me."

"Does anyone else know this?" I asked quietly.

He shook his head as tears rolled down his face. "I need you to tell me."

"What; what do you want to hear?" I questioned him in a stranger's voice. "You want to hear me say that I'm okay going to prison for a murder I didn't commit? That I'm here because you aren't man enough to take responsibility for your actions? That I forgive you for ruining my life?"

He tried to say something, but nothing came out. He cleared his throat again and eventually whispered, "Yes."

"Promise me I'll never see or hear from you again," I instructed him. He nodded his head, looking small as he sat hunched over. "Say it."

"Forgive me," he demanded again looking miserable.

"Say it!" I ordered, yelling at him as I stood up. The guards jerked up and started to move towards me, provoked to action by my unexpected behavior, but they held back to see what I'd do next.

"I promise I'll never bother you again," he choked out.

"You're forgiven," I said. Then I threw the phone down and walked away, leaving his pathetic memory behind me.

***

As I was escorted back to my little room, I knew that I really did forgive my step-dad. I had no place inside me for hatred to live and breed. Despite all that had happened, I still loved my mother and I forgave her. Surprisingly, I even forgave myself.

I didn't know if my step-dad would admit to his crimes. I don't think I really cared. I knew the truth and that was enough. I had been tormented thinking I had truly killed my mother. Believing I could do such a heinous thing had plagued my spirit. I couldn't recall any of the events that had transpired after my mother had stabbed me, but it was irrefutable that my finger prints were on the weapon. Though I had no memory of plunging the knife in, there'd been no doubt in my mind that I had pulled it out.

I hadn't defended myself at any point through the whole proceedings. There was no reason for me or anyone else to suspect anything other than my own guilt. If I myself couldn't be certain, without a doubt, that I hadn't killed my mother, I couldn't expect anyone else to believe it. I, along with everyone else, just accepted things as my step-dad had claimed them to be. No one had any reason to think otherwise.

His story had been logical. He had given the same account again and again, consistently reporting how he came into the room as I plunged the knife into my mother for the last time. He'd reported trying to help her with such feeling that it was touching, especially compared to my emotionless state. He played the distraught widower perfectly while I played the non-responsive psychopath with precision.

My step-dad's rendition of events was uncontested even by me and therefore, it became our truth. Truth I'd never be able to prove or change; truth that protected him from suspicion and penalty. Truth that I now knew was a lie.

Though my step-dad truly had assaulted my mother in the heat of passion, what he did to me was not. The crimes he perpetrated on me were done in cold blood. It hurt to realize that I had meant so little to him. Still, knowing this would make it easier for me to let him go, along with all the horrible memories of the life I left behind.

I was certain that my step-dad would have received a lesser punishment had he been honest about things, maybe even acquitted, but that time had passed. If someone learned the truth now, it would be a completely different story. My step-dad hadn't murdered my mom with premeditation, but he'd been extremely calculating in covering it up and taking my life from me.

My step-dad seemed to have everything wrapped up in a pretty little package. He thought he had covered all his bases and that he could move on with life, but he hadn't expected the dreams that haunted him. He never expected to feel guilty and he struggled with why he'd feel that way at all. He never had before, so why now?

I understood that his killing my mother was a physical manifestation of his guilt and regret. His decision to intervene and prevent her from killing me was a direct result of his impeded conscience. Of course, he had never really suffered from regret before, so he didn't understand or recognize it. I was surprised he felt anything even approaching remorse, so I would take that as a win in and of itself.

My step-dad had been shocked when he started to suffer from his guilt. He was tormented, as he thought he saw my mother everywhere he turned and he found he missed her terribly. He realized that his love for her would not diminish and that instead, he seemed to love her more. He turned her into a martyr and built her up in his mind to be even better in death than she'd been in life. This fabrication only added to his guilt and his sorrow.

My step-dad had thought that with my mother gone and me behind bars that he'd have a fresh start. He expected everything would go on and he'd be able to take the life insurance money and relocate, reinventing himself; starting life anew. He thought he'd be able to move beyond the past, but it wouldn't let go of him. It tormented him.

My step-dad was a shell of man. He was nothing without the strength of my mother. My mother had defined him and given him purpose. Now that she was gone, he realized that he was gone with her. He was lonely and he'd do anything to bring her back to him. As each day passed without her, he became more consumed by her memory and obsessed with reuniting with her. His plans faded into nothing, just as he was slowly being erased himself.

It had been difficult for me to look at him in the past. I lacked all respect for him, but I used to feel sorry for him. I realized that I had blamed my mother for his situation to some extent. Now, I saw him differently. Perhaps I could finally see him clearly for the first time. Now, I understood that he was the designer of his own circumstances due to the choices he'd made.

Thought it was painful to see him and to acknowledge him for who he truly was, I finally deemed him unworthy of my attention. Despite his kindness in coming to me and admitting his sins, I refused to feel sad for him; he'd done this to himself. I would not be held accountable for his actions and I wouldn't accept guilt for his wrong-doing; at least not the wrong he had inflected upon himself.

I no longer cared what people believed about my mother's death. It no longer mattered if they thought I had killed her or not; none of it mattered anymore because I finally knew. It was all I needed; to know that I hadn't succumbed to my dark impulses and given myself over to evil. Come what may, I could live with all things now that I knew I'd stayed true to myself; to the person I'd chosen to be. That was an unexpected gift from my step-dad.

No matter what my step-dad decided to do next, I felt justice had been served. If no one ever learned the truth and I stayed in prison forever, I'd be okay. I was grateful to learn that I hadn't murdered my mother; I had loved her and I loved her still. I hadn't wanted to hurt her and knowing with certainty that I hadn't harmed her gave me peace. I was thankful for that, even if no one else would ever know.

It was enough for me. It was enough to know who I really was. To face myself in my darkest hour and to retain my values was priceless. I hadn't given my soul away in vengeance or revenge. I had stayed true to myself even in the face of certain death. More so, I realized that in finding myself, my step-dad had discovered who he was, as well.

It was enough to know how he suffered. It made me happy to know that he finally saw himself for the pathetic, mindless peasant that he was. It was enough to see the realization in his eyes that no matter what he did or where he went, my mother would never love him the way he wanted her to; the way he loved her. It was enough that he knew he was nothing without her and nothing to me.

No matter what walls held me, I was no longer a prisoner to my mother, to my step-dad, or to my fear. My mother had lived and died by cruelty and lies. Both she and my step-dad had betrayed the ones they loved or should have loved. No matter how much space surrounded my step-dad, he'd always be crowded, smothered by his own insignificance. Justice had prevailed and I was at peace. It was indeed enough.

EPILOGUE

It wasn't long after my step-dad's visit that I received word of his death. He had hung himself, as cowards do. They found him hanging in his home, a suicide note near his body. The message he left behind simply said:

Tiffany,

I'm sorry. I waited too long to find the courage to help you. I see that now. I hope this letter will set you free.

I never meant to kill your mom. I just wanted to help you, but something happened when we were fighting and I just couldn't stop. I was angry and I stabbed her before I knew what I was doing.

In the end, I was too scared to tell the truth. I let you down again and I'm sorry. I shouldn't have let them blame you. Seeing you at the jail only made me feel worse.

I miss your mom every day. I didn't think it would hurt so much. All I want is to be with her so that's what I decided to do.

Sorry, Dad

I want to say that I felt sad or bad, but honestly, I just didn't feel anything. I felt empty. You know they say that love and hate are the opposite sides of the same coin. You don't feel love or hate, anger and joy if you don't care. They are all levels of passion. It isn't until that person is meaningless to you that you truly feel nothing. I guess I had achieved that lack of concern for my step-dad because I felt nothing.

It took a while for everything to filter through the system. It took a while before I could be released from the institution for the criminally insane. I didn't mind because I was still trying to make sense of my life; sense of what had happened. I wasn't sure how to reconcile my own feelings; though I wanted to forgive, I knew I'd never forget. The scarring was permanent.

Though I survived, I sustained incredible damage. Though the truth was finally known, acknowledged, and ultimately set me free, it wasn't the amazing relief I'd expected it to be. It was anticlimactic and really didn't seem to change much in the long run. It didn't stop the looks I got or the memories I carried. The truth may have been a key to my cell, but it wasn't the key to happiness I had always thought it'd be.

There was a hole that existed inside me; a hole that ached to be filled. I yearned for something I knew I'd never obtain; a mother who loved me and a family to welcome me home. I was alone and in more ways than one; in ways I'd never been before. I had nowhere to go and no one to return to; even Angie and Cedric had forsaken me. Though it was supposed to be a beginning, it felt more like an ending. I guess in truth it was an ending. I mean, it was the end of the life I knew and the person I had been.

I had finally been awoken from a horrible nightmare, but the shadows of that dream still caressed me. The emotions were still so strong and the events still too real. Though the door at the end of the long hall had finally been opened, it was a long walk to reach it. When I finally did, there was no telling what awaited me on the other side of the threshold.

The chain of abuse is so difficult to break and often repeats; continuing from generation to generation. I was afraid I wouldn't be strong enough to keep from becoming the person

my mother had been. Would I repeat the sins and perpetuate the pain? The fear was a constant companion; one that I
decided to use as a constant reminder.

I would not let my fear stop me. I had been strong enough to
accept death over murder, so I was strong enough to conquer
anything. I wouldn't let the old voices dictate me; I wouldn't
let anyone dictate who I was anymore. I was strong enough to
know who I was and I wasn't going to be beaten down again.

Even though there was a written confession proving my innocence, people watched me with suspicion. It was hard for
them to let go of what they'd believed to be true. Despite the
evidence, the truth was not the reality they had accepted.
They had difficulty trying to reconcile what they had thought
was real with what was now known was fact. I realized that
no amount of evidence was going to correct the image people
had of me.

I understood that people would struggle with who I really
was compared to what they'd assumed I'd been. They had
heard the stories too long and too loudly to reverse them.
Though they tried – God help them I could see they tried –
they failed. They failed and my presence would be a constant
reminder of their failure; my existence was in itself a confrontation with their own personal demons.

I would no longer be a person, but an example. Looking
at me, they'd constantly be reminded of their neglect; I'd be
the thorn in their side. When they saw me, they'd remember
how I had asked them for help and how they had chosen to
ignore me. They'd know how they had enabled my mother in
her pursuit to break me. I would be a constant reminder of
their guilt, their shame.

It was hard for people to look at me and they almost never
made direct eye contact. My history was rewritten overnight
and all the facts supported the story I had told from the beginning; the story no one listened to. What I represented was

more than they could take and people shied away from. This stigma alone would assure my place on the edge of society.

I wasn't sure what waited for me, as I stood on the steps of the prison that had been my shelter. As I took a moment to breathe the air in deeply and enjoy the breeze as it caressed my flesh, I rummaged through the options buzzing through my mind. Time would tell what would become of me, but I thought it'd be good to find a new place.

Life had taught me that there were many ways to die and various forms of death. In a sense, the girl I'd been had died that night alongside my mother. My essence transformed and carried on to this new person I'd become while in prison, but I wasn't the same. I didn't know this new me yet, but I hoped she'd be stronger than the girl I had left behind.

There were things I had to decide, but I wasn't sure what I'd do yet. To start with, I'd definitely move away from here and try to begin again; maybe I'd change my name. I didn't have any particular destination in mind and that was okay. I was okay. Standing in the wind, I felt empowered and I felt alive. Regardless of the scars I'd bear and no matter what wounds remained, I would survive. I had made it this far, hadn't I?

For now, I'd just walk out of the front gates and never look back. I would be grateful for the second chance I'd been given and I'd appreciate the life that urged me forward. The only thing I really knew was that from this moment on, I called the shots. I determined my own destiny. Come what may, I would be solely responsible for both the choices and the consequences of the decisions I made. For the first time in my life, I was truly free. I belonged to no body; I belonged to me.

ABOUT THE AUTHOR

J.M. Northup is an American author with the independent publisher, Creativia. She launched her writing career with her debut novel, *Fears of Darkness*, the first installment to *The Fears of Dakota* series. J.M. Northup released a novella of poetry entitled, *Soul Searching* and a second novel, *A Prisoner Within*. She continues to develop and research future projects.

4/16

Made in the USA
Charleston, SC
10 March 2016